Mac
on the
Road to
Marseille

Also by Christopher Ward
Mac in the City of Light

Mac on the Road to Marseille

Christopher Ward

DUNDURN
TORONTO

Editor: Allister Thompson
Design: Colleen Wormald
Cover design: Courtney Horner
Cover image credit: © Beastfromeast/iStockphoto
Printer: Webcom

Library and Archives Canada Cataloguing in Publication information is available

Ward, Christopher, author
        Mac on the road to Marseille / Christopher Ward. (The adventures of mademoiselle Mac ; 2)

Issued in print and electronic formats.
ISBN 978-1-4597-2188-3 (pbk.).--ISBN 978-1-4597-2189-0 (pdf).--
ISBN 978-1-4597-2190-6 (epub)
        I. Title. II. Series: Ward, Christopher. Adventures of mademoiselle Mac ; 2.

PS8645.A71M332 2015   jC813'.6   C2013-906078-2
                                               C2013-906079-0

1   2   3   4   5   19   18   17   16   15

 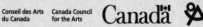 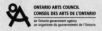

We acknowledge the support of the **Canada Council for the Arts** and the **Ontario Arts Council** for our publishing program. We also acknowledge the financial support of the **Government of Canada** through the **Canada Book Fund** and **Livres Canada Books**, and the **Government of Ontario** through the **Ontario Book Publishing Tax Credit** and the **Ontario Media Development Corporation**.

Visit us at
Dundurn.com | @dundurnpress | Facebook.com/dundurnpress | Pinterest.com/Dundurnpress

Dundurn
3 Church Street, Suite 500
Toronto, Ontario, Canada
M5E 1M2

To Sarah
reader, teacher, sister

One

Once again, he shifted his aching body within the cramped space of the electrical closet — slowly, very slowly so as not to make a sound. He listened to the last receding footsteps echoing past the medieval moat in the underground section of the former castle. The clatter of visitors' voices gradually diminished as Monday's closing time approached, and he was left with the sound of his own breathing and the prickly heat on the skin under his clothes. He waited, aware that one inopportune cough or that sneeze that had been taunting him for hours could derail everything. After a cautious length of time had passed and a tomblike silence settled on the old fortress, he pulled a penlight from his overalls and, careful not to allow any light to escape beneath the door, shone it on the electrical panel inches from his face.

He knew this panel like it was a musical instrument he had mastered, and probably could have carried out his task in darkness, but he took no chances given what was at stake. The route from the basement to Room 6 of the Denon Wing was as familiar as the layout of his own apartment. He also knew well that, thanks to the strike, a certain looseness prevailed among the substitute staff during the security shift changeover and that the regularity of the previous false alarms had further dulled the response effort. He made his move, disabling alarms, security monitors, and key tracking beams that acted as motion detectors, covering his route to Room 6 on the second floor. He attached the fake beard that instantly aged him and pulled on the cap that made him unrecognizable. Cane in hand, he exited the closet with great relief and made his way swiftly down the darkened hallway, slowing to a hobble as he passed flustered security officers, taking in their pitying glances at the creaky old janitor as they rushed by.

Taking the stairs past the majestic Winged Victory sculpture, which a few hours ago had been surrounded by noisy crowds of tourists posing and snapping photos they would probably never look at, he approached a cluster of guards, arguing and shining flashlights at each other. Once he had passed by, all but invisible, he unscrewed the top of his cane and pulled out a small fogging device. He smiled as the gunshot sound effects from his phone boomed in the stone stairwell, causing instant panic. Trailing fog, he moved toward Room 6 as everyone else raced to the stairwell and the source of the supposed gunfire. Once inside Room 6, behind a veil of fog, he stopped briefly and glanced at the jewel of the great Louvre Museum, the *Mona Lisa*. She probably hadn't been this alone in a century, he mused. He was as familiar with her face as anyone in the art world, so without dwelling further on her mystery, he hastily removed the side of her glass case and carefully extracted the world's most famous painting. From the shaft of his cane he unrolled her near twin, expertly installed the work, and replaced the glass case before gently rolling up da Vinci's original and sliding it into the tube nestled inside his cane.

An hour later, the gendarmes were satisfied that nothing was missing and no damage had been done, and the only mysteries were the smell of fog, now scattered, and the sound of gunfire, now disputed. They were more annoyed at the repeated security alerts and the incompetence of the strike-breaking substitute guards. Minus his overalls, wig, and fake beard, he stepped out under the arcade of the Richelieu wing, lit a Gitane cigarette and spotted one of the waiters at the Café Marley.

"*Bonsoir*, Monsieur. Follow me."

"*Bonsoir*, Gilles."

"Another false alarm?"

"*Oui*, I'm afraid so. The fourth this week, or is it the fifth? This darned strike."

"Your customary *noisette*, Monsieur?"

"*Oui, merci*, and a tiny Armagnac as well."

"*Bien sûr*. An occasion?"

"Yes, I'm celebrating a perfect September evening, Gilles."

Two

"You should never ask 'Do you want *more* tea? It suggests gluttony," asserted Penelope, "just 'Would you like some tea?'"

She pretended to pour a thimble-sized cup for a stuffed mouse dressed as a ballerina. I knew it was up to me to serve imaginary slices of lemon cake to an expectant Hop the kangaroo, Norm the bunny, and my personal favourite, the long-suffering Bussi the chimp. As Penelope looked on critically, I performed my duties with an experienced hand. I pushed out of my mind the fact that we were many years removed from this sort of thing and concentrated on paying off my debt to Penelope for leaving her at the mercy of Mademoiselle Lesage for a week last summer in Paris while I tried to save the city from perpetual darkness and the destruction of its most important historical monuments. Really!

I knew that the slightest resistance on my part could bring out the doll wedding finery.

"Bussi, more ... I mean, would you care for a spot of tea, old boy?"

Penelope's eyes narrowed; I was on shaky ground here, although a part of me suspected she was long since done with the tea parties of our preschool years and was just torturing me because she could. I also wanted to borrow her safety pin bracelet, the only cool piece of jewellery she owned as far as I was concerned, for my return trip to Paris. Penelope, as usual, read my mind.

"You used to love doing the special menus as I recall, Mackenzie."

I winced. Only Penelope at her most superior and my grandpa could get away with calling me anything but Mac. I also used to love the Playdough hair salon, too. Penelope sighed and got up, signalling the end of our fourth tea party this week.

"So, what do you need for your trip? If you didn't borrow anything, you wouldn't have any luggage. How about my cute little pirate blouse and the leather vest with the big buttons?"

"Umm, how about the bracelet that Gerald gave you," I said meekly, referring to Penelope's first real boyfriend.

(Let it be acknowledged that the boyfriend concept was foreign to me. There were some maybes, a couple of could bes, but no wannabes that I knew of.)

"*Pas de problème*," said Penelope, pulling it out of a giant jewellery box and holding it out. She pulled it back just as quickly and eyed me suspiciously. "As long as you don't wear it with corduroy, denim, or anything Pippi Longstocking would be seen in."

That covered my entire wardrobe, unfortunately, but when I pictured the Russian Church on rue Daru in Paris, done up for a wedding, I knew she had a point. Dutifully being Penelope's paper doll, I suffered through a frilly fashion parade till we settled on a simple velvet dress, short jacket, and boots that pinched like crazy, but which I had to admit looked pretty cool. She slipped the bracelet in place and stepped back.

"*Voilà*! Not bad at all."

Looking at myself, I suppressed a grin and said, "Okay, if you say so, Madame Chanel."

"I see a young tousle-haired Parisian *garçon* with a shy smile in your future, Mac."

"Right. Hey, let's get our bikes, go to the top of the canyon, and race all the way down through Lower Mandeville. We haven't done that in ages."

Penelope closed her eyes and slowly exhaled. "I'll have Daddy deliver your outfit before you leave tomorrow. I'm pretty sure my bike's got a flat."

Fashion — *la mode*, as they call it in Paris — had eluded me completely. My mom and Penelope's efforts had gone to waste; they might form a support group any day. My mom says every wardrobe needs basics and a few "statement" pieces. My statement is "I couldn't care less." Or is it "I *could* care less"? I can never remember. Mind you, I *do* appreciate scarves, thanks to Sashay, the bride-to-be, and the fact that a scarf pretty much saved my life. There's a great ad here: "Stylish! Warm! And it prevents you from tumbling to your death from the spiky rooftop of a twelfth-century Gothic cathedral. On sale now!" But that's another story, one you may already know if you heard about my first trip to The City of Light.

Three

We made it, no thanks to my parents. At the end of a packing frenzy, my mom had to sit on her suitcase. To no avail, my dad tried his best tactics. "Where are you going to put all the cool stuff you buy at the Bon Marché?"

My mom had to step in when my dad tried out his French on the check-in person at American Airlines. "*Voici, ma femme. Voici ma fille. Voici les billets de ma femme et ma fille.*"

My mom did the hissing stage whisper voice. "They don't speak the language of every destination, you know."

Dressed in seasonal finery, Paris looked like a different city than the one I'd seen six months earlier, but just as magical. The seventh arrondisement, one of the twenty districts that make up the French capital, was decorated in dreamy blue and green lights over the narrow streets and there was hardly a Santa in sight. We stayed at the oh-so-cool Hôtel Costes on rue Faubourg St. Honoré in the heart of the fashion district, beautifully decorated and so ready to welcome my mom's credit card. My dad was excited about the chilled out DJ compilations from the hotel. I cannot lie, I loved the window displays at the Galeries Lafayette and le Printemps on Boulevard Haussmann, and I happily reclaimed kidhood and stood on the little ramp they set up so the tykes can see the mechanical twirling bears and ballerinas. Penelope would be in ecstasy. We skated in front of the Hôtel de Ville, overlooking the Seine. My mom and dad held hands and whispered to each other.

On Christmas Eve we made our way to the Cathédral Alexander Nevsky, the Russian church on rue Daru, for Rudee and Sashay's wedding. The side street was jammed with taxis all the way to the Parc Monceau and around the Place des Ternes as Rudee's fellow cab driver pals, including his best friend and bandmate, François "Dizzy" Caboche, came to celebrate the occasion they all would have bet heavily could never happen.

Lit by hundreds of candles, the church was packed with a colourful collection of Parisiennes: the riverbank booksellers, known as the *bouquinistes*, the waiters and waitresses from the bistros and brasseries, and, of course, the cabbies with their wives, husbands, kids, and one extra-large *bouvier* named Odile. Sashay's theatrical friends were dressed in capes and chapeaux, in velvet, satin, and sequins in blinding burgundies, shades of saffron and iridescent blue, and of course wearing scarves, Sashay's trademark. The river rats, Rudee's pals from the waterfront, seemed to have made the most effort to rise to the occasion, done up in spiffy nautical gear, not a one to be seen chewing tobacco. Blag LeBoeuf wandered in late, rolling his eyes at the grandness of the setting, but it was his date, Tawdry, who owned the spotlight during their entrance, balancing on six-inch heels attached to leopard print thigh-highs and a form-fitting shiny black off-the-shoulder gown. In the tiny sanctuary of the church, playing a relatively sedate version of "La Vie en Rose," The Hacks, Rudee's band minus Rudee, wearing matching pink tuxedos, dropped a couple of beats at the sight of Blag's date. I sat with my mom in the front pew alongside Magritte, the stylish Parisian police inspector, and Madeleine, the taxi dispatcher, whose wheelchair was decorated in ribbons and roses. We watched with pride as my dad filled in admirably on organ for Rudee, who was otherwise occupied, cursing to himself in his little apartment above the church, hastily sucking mints to cover his beet breath and tweaking his formidable comb-over into wedding day helmet form.

The ceremony went off without a hitch — oh, wait a minute, they did get hitched! The Hacks wobbled through a spirited version of the Wedding March. Rudee beamed and Sashay performed an impromptu twirl down the aisle to oohs and ahhs, spinning her wedding veil like the scarves in her gypsy dance. Rudee's enthusiastic "Do I!" response during the vows broke up the room.

Afterward, my dad had his arm around my mom, gliding her towards Dizzy's cab. "Wasn't that romantic, honey?"

"Hmm-mmm. Kind of like that movie *La Belle et la Bête*." We'd watched the original *Beauty and the Beast* in French class one time when our teacher had laryngitis, and it *was* kind of romantic, but I think my mom's comment had another intention.

"Never thought I'd see the day." My dad smiled and shook his head. "And I understand that Rudee is moving into Sashay's place until they find something of their own."

"Sashay has declared her apartment a beet-free zone," I informed them, "with cooked cabbage only on Saturdays."

"*Allons-y mes amis Americains*!" said Dizzy with a flourish as we approached his car, parked in the cluster of cabs outside the church. My mom eyed the trombone-shaped exhaust pipes and paisley interior with suspicion.

The Café Taxi, shortened to CAFTA thanks to a couple of burned-out bulbs, was decorated in a scarf motif in honour of the bride, transforming the place into a gauzy supper club, tables pushed to the sides with an area for dancing and mingling set up in the middle. In one corner there was a small stage for The Hacks to perform on. Would Rudee play his own wedding party?

My parents were clearly mystified by the reception I received as we wove through the crowd, where I was greeted by cabbies, many of whose names I didn't know.

"Little Mac, *allo*!"

"There she is!"

"Welcome back, *la petite acrobate*!"

Dizzy had been charged with keeping a lid on my Bastille Day exploits from last summer. I introduced the parents to Mink Maynard, the rhyming drummer and vocalist for Rudee's band, The Hacks.

"Mademoiselle Mac, I'm glad you're back."

Mink and my dad were soon deep into musician talk. "I hear you guys are doing some of the old songs that Rudee and I wrote back in the day."

"Hey King Daddy, what do you say, let's jam tonight, so I can hear you play," Mink said, using my dad's old band nickname.

Just as the band was setting up on the stage, Sashay and Rudee arrived to cheers and whistles. Rudee rushed to the stage and grabbed the microphone.

"Hello, partypants!" he shouted. "*Merci, mes amis* and a special thank-you to my friends who flapped here from America." Rudee shot me a smile and I managed a little wave back. "My fellow *chauffeurs*, I no longer have to spend my nights drinking your tar coffee and listening to your wind up my sleeves." This classic Rudee-ism brought a roar of laughter from the room and an expression of disbelief and amusement from my mom. Rudee pressed on, at times incomprehensibly. "From this foot forward, I will be with my Queen of Dreams, Sashay D'Or! So let's unwrap this party, toast my beautiful bride, and dance until the cabs come home!"

It became as wild and celebratory an occasion as anyone could have wished. My mom and I cheered loudly when my dad sat in for Rudee with The Hacks and performed "Transatlantic Train" and something called "Onion Heart." This was topped only by Rudee doing the organ solo in "Gâteaux to Go" with his nose. Madeleine followed this up by wheeling her chair through the crowd to present the lucky couple with a wedding cake in the shape of a giant beet, in honour of Rudee's deep love of "the king of vegetables." Fortunately for Sashay, and all concerned, the icing was strawberry.

Dizzy asked me to dance, and I was glad my lack of coordination was covered up by his free-form craziness on the dance floor. He caught me smiling.

"I call this 'the tree,'" he said, and I could picture the waving arms as branches.

"Nice! Great party." I looked around CAFTA at the full-on merriment. "Think you can top this for New Year's?"

"Funny you should mention that," said Dizzy, twirling around like he was at some hippie folk festival. "Every New Year's there's an annual taxi road rally. This year it's hosted by the Marseille Marauders, the nastiest lot of drivers you've ever seen. After forty-eight hours of driving the back roads, the race ends up on their home turf."

As fascinating as this was, I had a feeling Dizzy had a reason for telling me this right now. I nodded with as serious an expression as possible given that we were on a dance floor and my partner, a full-grown man, was waving his arms Indian god-style, doing "the tree." To say nothing of the fact that his best friend had recently performed an organ solo with his nose. At his own wedding.

"The Marauders' advantage is mighty, given that the trouble-making spectators are almost as bad as the drivers and the road conditions." Dizzy gave his head a little shake like he was trying to dislodge a bee. "Their leader is Margot Mallard, a most unsavoury woman." Dizzy's lip curled at the thought. "Our team, the Parisian Partypoppers ... Rudee's idea —" I figured " — won last year, and at our victory party at the Arc de Triomphe, the Marauders vowed revenge."

"This sounds amazing, Dizzy, I wish I could be there to cheer you on."

"Yes..." Dizzy paused and pursed his lips. "Madeleine has chosen the three drivers and their three navigators, and this year she assigned Rudee to be Blag's guide, as a symbol of *solidarité*, given that they decided to forgive and forget their long, stormy past."

"I hope Rudee keeps his cool," I said. "How is he with directions?"

"Welllll ..." said Dizzy, "last year, one of the clues involved a 'fork in the road,' and Rudee was convinced it was a lunch stop ... you can imagine."

I could. "Yes, I get the picture." I strongly sensed there was more to come.

"Hmmm, yes ... but it's a somewhat bigger picture," he said, looking around to see who might be listening. "You see, Sashay booked their honeymoon on a Mediterranean cruise ship, leaving tomorrow and returning January second to Nice." Dizzy eyed me with a serious expression, no longer dancing "the tree."

"But Rudee will miss the rally," I said.

"*Exactement*," replied Dizzy.

"And Blag won't have a navigator."

"*Précisement*."

"And no other driver in his right mind would agree to drive with Blag."

"*Absolument*."

"And you're thinking ..."

"*Vraiment*."

Really? I thought. Dizzy didn't look like he was joking, even slightly. "Surely Americans aren't eligible."

"*Normalement, non*. But you were given the Pomme Verte by Magritte last year, the highest honour for a non-French citizen."

"Yes, *vraiment*."

"And after your adventures in the underground together, you and Blag are friends."

"*Absolument*."

"And you couldn't possibly say no to your old pal Rudee Daroo, especially on his wedding night."

"*Exactement*," I answered mechanically. "No, wait! Dizzy, this is crazy. I can't do this."

"Why not? You would provide a considerable weight advantage, particularly if you weren't wearing a heavy metal bracelet." Dizzy indicated Penelope's safety pin jewellery. "At the very least you'd serve to counterbalance Blag's weight disadvantage."

"I've got a flight in two days. And I have a holiday reading list for school. And my best friend Penelope's birthday party. And my mom would never let me do this in a million years. Did I mention my occasional bouts of motion sickness ... half the time I was in Rudee's cab, I had my head between my knees practicing my mom's yoga breathing."

"Yes, the smell of beets while in motion will occasionally induce nausea."

It took a second before he laughed and I realized he was joking, but only about the last part.

"Dizzy, I'm sorry."

He smiled and held up his hand. "It's okay, Mademoiselle Mac. I understand. Rudee will understand. Blag will be fine — he'd probably rather be on his own."

"I feel really badly, Dizzy, but I just can't be in the road rally."

"It's fine. By the way, did my dancing make you dizzy?" I laughed and he started up with "the tree" once more, so I joined in enthusiastically.

I'd only seen Sashay from afar this evening, and even though last summer's events had made us close, she now seemed as mysterious as ever. Whether she was walking down the aisle at the Russian church, dancing circles around a spellbound Rudee at CAFTA, or turning her head to take her vows, her movements were gracious and mesmerizing. I'd seen her take an audience vividly back to their childhood days with her gypsy dance of dreams, and I wondered if she was living out her own dream today. She surprised me by throwing a scarf across my eyes from behind, but I knew from the lavender scent who it was. She embraced me and held me with her eyes as only Sashay can.

"My little Mac, you are not so little it seems. Fifteen now?"

I smiled and nodded. "Congratulations, Sashay, I'm so happy for you and Rudee. He really is the sweetest man in the world."

"As long as he avoids those peasant vegetables, *ma cherie.*" Her eyes twinkled. "Yes, my Rudee is sweet. Today he called me his little cabbage cake. So romantic."

"Speaking of romantic, I hear that you and Rudee are going on a Mediterranean cruise for your honeymoon."

"Yes, I've always wanted to see Capri, Sorrento, Napoli." Her eyes closed with the delight of it all. "Rudee had proposed a visit to the Dobinska Ice Caves in Slovakia, but I didn't want him to spoil me too much."

"I guess a girl wants to save something to dream about."

"*Oui, c'est ça.*"

We both scanned the room, simultaneously spotting two ridiculous sights. Rudee and my dad, arms overlapped, were both playing furious accompaniment to "Stinkbomb Serenade" and laughing uncontrollably like a couple of adult children. Almost as absurd was the scene on the dance floor where Dizzy and my mom were doing a *pas de deux* tree-style, looking like the twelve-armed Indian dancers. Ewww! Sashay began to imitate them, and before long, we were holding on to each other, shaking with laughter. They spotted us, came over, and we all found a table.

"Mom, this Sashay."

"Oh Sashay, *enchanté*. That's the right word, isn't it?"

"Yes, of course, and I'm charmed to meet you as well. I have such a place in my heart for your remarkable daughter."

I tried to shoot her the *Yikes. Danger. Go no further* look, but it ended well.

"She has such a sophisticated appreciation for French culture."

"*Merci*," my mom replied a bit awkwardly. "Well, I guess she'll be getting even more immersed, thanks to François."

Oh, it's François now that Dizzy's in full charm offensive mode. What's up here? I wondered. My mom gave me that glazed "oh to be young again" expression.

"Mac, what a wonderful opportunity to see the picturesque countryside in the south of France on the auto rally. Oh, the charming little villages, stopping to pick blueberries, girls on *bicyclettes* with baguettes in their baskets ... oh."

I was speechless through this recitation as Dizzy, or François, maintained a look of angelic innocence until Sashay interrupted.

"Are you talking about the New Year's taxi rally? It's a crazy —"

Dizzy cut in abruptly. "Yes, I agree, Mac would be crazy to miss it."

Sashay looked perplexed. "But the driving is wild —"

"Oh, I know how wild about the drivers people become," said Dizzy, winking at me. Sashay just shook her head.

I shot daggers at him but realized that now my mom had been sold, I couldn't unsell her and ruin Rudee and Sashay's honeymoon. Could I?

The Hacks took a break and Rudee and my dad joined us, basking in the praise for their impromptu duet. At that moment a very serious Magritte approached our table, bowler hat in hand and customary umbrella tucked under his arm.

"Mesdames, messieurs, it is with regret that I must leave you to your celebration. A serious crime of utmost cultural significance has been committed."

Cultural crime? Was someone caught not rolling their r's on French television? Did the pastry maker at Ladurée sell unflaky croissants? We all waited for Magritte to provide details.

"It has been discovered that the *Mona Lisa* is a fake." The silence at our table was monumental. "Yes, da Vinci's masterwork, *La Joconde*, or the portrait of Lisa Gherardini, the wife of Francesco del Giocondo, has been identified as a counterfeit, albeit a very good one that captures the enigmatic expression of the subject in the original with a close approximation of the creator's use of *sfumato*." Magritte nodded at the stunned expression on his little audience and looked away pensively. "*Sfumato*, of course, refers not only to da Vinci's brilliant brush stroke technique, but also to the seemingly conflicting notion of contemplating two opposing ideas simultaneously."

The O of Rudee's mouth could have accommodated a pineapple ring. "But Magritte, how long has the phoney Mona been dangling in the Louvre?"

Good question, if a little strangely put, I thought.

"This is difficult to ascertain, *mon ami*. During war times she has been taken to safety in various locations, and of course she was stolen in 1911 and missing for two years, thanks to a mad Italian motivated by a disturbed form of patriotism. But there are aspects to the matter which must remain classified for the moment."

We all began talking at once in hushed tones. "So, how did they figure out that it's not the real *Mona Lisa*?" I asked Magritte.

"Ah, mademoiselle, that is the heart of the matter. You see, *La Joconde* has acquired, unexpectedly, an accessory, most modern. But I must investigate at the scene."

"Let me take you to the Louvre," said Rudee, "that is, if my wife approves." He beamed at Sashay, who wordlessly nodded. "With all the partypoppers not driving, you couldn't find a cab for all the china on the map."

"*Merci*, Rudee," said Magritte.

"Could I come with you?" Nothing ventured, nothing tried, as Rudee once said. I looked to my mom and dad but they seemed too astounded to object.

Magritte steepled his fingers contemplatively and after a lengthy pause said, "*Pourquoi pas*? Why not? Have you ever seen the *Mona Lisa*?"

When I said no, Magritte replied, "I believe we could use a set of fresh eyes on this brazen crime. *Allons-y*."

Four

I held my breath more than once as Rudee negotiated the pretzel-like streets of Montmartre, around the beautiful Sacre Coeur church on the hill, and careened toward the rue de Rivoli, where the Louvre was located. Magritte sat in meditative silence in the back seat so we didn't speak, but I could hear the agitation in Rudee's breathing. We approached the museum through the Carousel de Louvre, past the posh shops, now closed, that lined the way.

A mere nod from Magritte eased us past the museum security and various other authorities on the way to the second floor. The policeman's leisurely pace allowed me to check out the extraordinary art as we passed, but it was the vastness of the place that awed me. I knew from French class that it had been a fortress, once housing royalty and all their wigs and stuff, but you could comfortably play Quidditch in the high-ceilinged halls.

As we approached the Denon wing of the museum and the room that had been Mona Lisa's home for many years, I could feel the tension rising. We were greeted by the director of the Louvre, Blaise Roquefort, a small, intense man in an elegant black suit wearing a scowl that would make Mona stop smiling if she were there. He nodded to Magritte, eyed Rudee with suspicion, and treated me to the briefest of lip curls, as only the French can do.

He spoke through clenched teeth. "This is supposed to be impossible, Magritte. I don't have to tell you the level of security that surrounds this cursed masterpiece. She is protected like the Crown Jewels or the American president. She's never alone."

Magritte nodded sagely as they approached the famous painting.

"When I took over, this great institution was a mess under DeFaux. There was a strike, the windows of the pyramid were filthy. And they were serving Belgian wine — no offence, Magritte — in the cafeteria. Belgian!"

Magritte arched a sympathetic eyebrow. Roquefort was trembling now. "The flaw ... the alteration ... this distortion was discovered by a ..." His nose twitched like he'd discovered something stinky in the back of the fridge, "... a teenager."

He didn't say "no offence" to me. Oh well. I found myself reacting like I was seeing the original, not a supreme fake. It's so small; she's not really smiling; what's going on behind her — the usual observations. At this point Monsieur Roquefort crumbled like a delicate blue cheese.

"Magritte, I will be crucified by the art world. I have had this job less than three months. It is my life's dream. Arghhh." With this, the director buried his head in his hands and wept uncontrollably.

Rudee and I looked at each other uncomfortably, and he shrugged. Magritte approached the case, still guarded by a pair of expressionless guards, and extracted a magnifying glass. He was having a Sherlock moment.

A series of mmm's, ahh's, and ooo's were followed by a couple of ah ha's and one prominent "*Zut alors*!" An astounded "*Mon Dieu*!" finished off Magritte's observations.

"*Incroyable! Mes amis*, come and have a look."

Roquefort continued sniffling in the background as we huddled around phoney Mona.

"What is it, Monsieur Magritte?" I whispered, aware of the seriousness of the moment.

"Look at *La Joconde*'s right wrist. What do you see emerging from the sleeve of her garment?"

"Her arm, Magritte!" Rudee said excitedly, before his expression clouded. "But what else would it be?"

"*Oui*, but look again. There is the hint of something shiny on her arm."

We all leaned in together, noses pressed to the glass protecting the painting.

"Cool!" I said before realizing the complete inappropriateness of this observation. "She's wearing a watch."

"So, Mona Lisa was not timeless," said Rudee, sounding very pleased with himself and rendering my comment forgettable.

"Ah, but the wristwatch did not exist in Renaissance Italy." Magritte raised his eyebrows. "A Swiss invention, I believe, a Monsieur Patek Philippe in the late nineteenth century. Although the French, typically, have disputed this claim, preferring to point to a Louis Cartier, who developed a watch for an associate who was working in the early aviation industry." Rudee looked ready to go Vesuvius on Magritte, who continued his droning aside. "Of course, even if Leonardo is credited with inventing the first clock with separate hour and minute mechanisms, using springs rather than weights, the wristwatch, which I should mention was only for women at the time, came a good four hundred years after da Vinci created the exquisite wrist of *La Joconde*."

He'd totally lost me, so I turned my focus to Mona's four-hundred-year-old wrist. "A Fossil!" I observed, a little loudly.

"No, *ma petite*," Magritte chuckled patronizingly, "although I admire your interest in palaeontology, a fossil would customarily be remains that had been around for at least ten thousand years, and this bauble is considerably more recent."

"No, I mean a Fossil watch, a Stella mini. They're really cool right now, or *chouette* as you guys say; my friend Penelope is really hoping to get one for her birthday."

Monsieur Roquefort did one of those wet, snuffling sobs with a little squeak at the end. It echoed off the walls of Room 6. We ignored him and continued to stare at Mona's new bling.

Magritte pursed his lips in deep contemplation and Rudee shook his head, confused. "Well, for flying out cloud."

Five

In the days following the Mona discovery, the press had a field day. CRIME TIME blared the *Le Devoir* newspaper in bold letters. MONA BALOGNA said *Le Figaro*, and in an exclusive interview with *Art World*, the former director of the Louvre, Raoul DeFaux, recently replaced in a power struggle, hastened to point out that this heinous assault on beauty and history would never have occurred while he was director. "Not on my watch," said the saucy quote! Speculation on the motive for the theft, as much as on the identity of the perpetrator, ran wild in Paris. Every Métro car rumbling between stations, every park bench decorated by pigeons, every café steaming with witty conversation was abuzz with the subject. Christmas came a distant second.

Except in a certain hotel room at the Hôtel Costes. I'd been so energized by the wedding, the party, and especially the trip to the Louvre, that I couldn't sleep, so in Penelope's honour I cut out paper angels and hung them across the room. After a festive and extremely cream-filled holiday breakfast, my mom and dad were in a serious post-pastry pre-nap stupor. I was getting restless, all that sugar having had the opposite effect on me, when my brand new, ultra-cool cell phone rang with my signature tune, "Taxi Girl" by Zen Garage. It was too early to be Penelope, who was no doubt deep asleep in Lower Mandeville nine time zones away.

"*Joyeux Noël*, Mademoiselle Mac!" Rudee sang out. "Did Snappy Claus come to your hotel room with his eight tiny oxen last night?"

I laughed and mouthed "Rudee" to the 'rents, who were rapidly losing the eyelid wars.

"Don't you and Sashay have to be on your way to Nice soon?" I asked, taking an opportunity to check the time on my new phone.

"Yes, that's why I'm calling you, little Mac. Dizzy wants you to see us off at the air salon."

"Hang on, Rudee." I gave the bed a little shake. "Rudee wants to know if I can see them off. Dizzy's driving."

"Sure, honey," my mom mumbled, "say *au revoir* for me."

"And *bon appetit*," my dad managed before passing out.

I hung up and grabbed my new and also ultra-cool pink denim jacket and Penelope's bracelet, reasoning that the colour would lessen my fashion crime in her eyes. Waving to two sets of sleeping feet, I closed the door gently and headed for the street, wondering why the hallway of our totally chic hotel had to look like an abandoned tunnel.

Paris hadn't been able to manage a white Christmas, but the pearly grey rain didn't dampen the dreamy beauty of the rue Faubourg St. Honoré. A few *flaneurs*, as the French refer to their aimless strollers, ambled past the holiday windows of the shops. The spell was broken by the arrival of Dizzy's cab in front of the hotel. Bertrand, the doorman, pretended not to notice the trombone-shaped exhaust pipes as he held the door for me.

Sashay and Rudee were cuddling in the back and Dizzy and I exchanged bemused looks.

"Well, well, well," said Dizzy with a raised eyebrow, "the famous Hôtel Costes. Does the thirty-euro *croissant amande* taste better?"

"Not sure about that, but it's definitely cool. Johnny Depp was in the bar last night surrounded by a herd of towering model types. I couldn't actually see him but I did take a photo on my new phone of the place where he was standing last night. Look!"

"No talking about pirates, please," said Rudee, "we're going to be sailing on a cruise control ship for a week, and you know the stories."

I could never be sure if Rudee was aware of his wacky Rudee-isms or not, but I had to admit they were making more and more sense to me. Was this a good thing?

"I have one '*au revoir*' and one '*bon appetit*,' which I think was supposed to be a '*bon voyage*,' to deliver. Oh yes, and a '*bonne Noël*' from me."

"*Merci*, Mac," said Sashay, "and I have *un petit cadeau* for you." She handed me a slender silver package with a bow tied to resemble a rose. *The French certainly know about presentation*, I thought. Inside was a delicate scarf, also in silver, with a wing-like pattern in rose that went perfectly with my outfit *du jour*. Good heavens, listen to me. When did clothing become an "outfit"? I was sounding way too much like Penelope. Next I'd be scanning the sidewalks and cafés for tousle-haired *garçons*.

"*Bonjour, mes chauffeurs!*" Madeleine's crusty voice crackled through the taxi radio, sounding not at all like her normally cheery self. "I have distressing news. Another of our national treasures has been discovered to be a fake. There is a swarm of flies at the D'Orsay investigating. *Mon Dieu*. What next, *mes amis*?" With a tone of exasperation, she signed off. "Try to have a *joyeux Noël*."

"Dizzy," Rudee said forcefully, "we must see for our own selves."

"But what can we do?" said Dizzy. "And what about your flight?" He glanced at Sashay in the rear-view mirror, hoping to appeal to her good sense. She pursed her lips in the famous French "*moue*," as they called it, her good sense telling her that it was useless to oppose Rudee at this moment. I sat in silence in the passenger seat, knowing where this was going, and more than a little curious to see the Musée D'Orsay, which I'd missed on my last trip to Paris.

"No sweating, Dizzy," said Rudee, "take rue de Rivoli all the way. It's empty like a bird's nest on Christmas Day."

"Sweet. We could drive by the Louvre, right?" Dizzy glared at me. "I love the I.M. Pei pyramid!"

"That's right, Mac." Rudee beamed with pride at my taxi drivers' knowledge of Paris. "You see, Dizz, how she will steer Blag in the rally."

"Hmmm, yes, I hope. Might I mention that the Orly airport is in the opposite direction?" Dizzy tried to get Rudee's attention but was ignored, so he shrugged and hit the accelerator, sending a twin blast of exhaust into the quiet Paris morning.

The Musée D'Orsay, a former train station, is a beautiful Left Bank landmark, across the river from the Tuileries Gardens and an éclair's throw from the Eiffel Tower. The third floor of the museum houses the world's most amazing collection of Impressionist paintings — Cezannes and Monets rub shoulders with Toulouse-Lautrec's and the portrait of Whistler's mom. Is my French art appreciation class showing? Something told me that this was where we were heading, and I felt excitement at seeing it mixed with dread at the thought of what a thief might have made off with.

Rudee avoided the growing scrum in front of the main entrance and confidently guided us toward a rear door. Inside, the great hall of the old train station was empty, but it was easy to imagine it filled with travellers at the beginning of the twentieth century. Now it held an incredible collection of sculpture by Rodin, the guy who created *The Thinker* and others. A lone gendarme stood at the bottom of the stairs to the upper floors. He met Rudee with a stony expression.

"*Oui?*"

"Magritte," said Rudee with an equally serious look as he flashed something from his pocket. The guard, eyeing us suspiciously, allowed this odd group to pass. He couldn't resist a glance of admiration at Sashay as she whisked past in a lavender breeze.

"What did you show him?" I asked.

Rudee grinned slyly and showed me a business card with a picture of a man in a suit and bowler hat with an apple in front of his face. Okay, weird, I thought, but ...

"The Belgian artist, Rene Magritte's self-portrait. Only Inspector Magritte's closest friends have one," Rudee said proudly. "Here, Mac, you squeeze on to this one."

Magritte was in full contemplation, hands clasped behind his back, when we got to the third floor of the D'Orsay. Small groups of officials, police, and museum employees hovered, nervously whispering amongst themselves. I looked around in awe at an entire room dedicated to the paintings of the Dutch genius, Vincent Van Gogh. *Starry Night*, the couple sleeping in the hay, the self-portraits — I'd seen them all in books, but seeing them in front of my eyes was something else. Magritte stood motionless in front of one of the most famous of all the works, Van Gogh's *Bedroom in Arles*, a painting of his humble little room with its table and chairs, a pitcher, a towel, and the bed with its red blanket and ... hey, I'd never noticed that before.

Dizzy, Rudee, and Sashay seemed befuddled as Magritte arched an eyebrow, steepled his fingers, and slowly leaned in toward the canvas.

"Isn't that cute, there's a little chocolate on the pillow," I exclaimed a bit too loudly, realizing in that moment that there should not be a chocolate on the pillow of the bed of Van Gogh's *Bedroom in Arles*. Definitely not.

Magritte closed his eyes and nodded rhythmically. "*Oui*, Mademoiselle Mac, *un petit chocolat*...."

I leaned in next to Magritte for a closer look. "In the shape of an earlobe," I whispered, slowly making the connection with the legendary tale of the artist cutting off a piece of his own ear in a fit of madness.

Dizzy, Rudee, and Sashay stood, mouths agape, like children waiting for a little Christmas bonbon to be deposited on their tongues.

Six

By the dim light in the cool of the ancient wine cellar, a trim, grey-haired man in his mid-sixties navigated his way past rack upon rack of some of the finest vintage wines in the country. They were arranged by the glorious regions of France and the individual vineyards that had produced the grapes, from the Loire, Alsace, and the mighty B's, Bordeaux, Burgundy, and Beaujolais. Pausing to be sure he was alone, he shifted a crate of Rhone Rosé, now filled with empty bottles, to one side. What appeared to be a wall of ancient brick concealed something else, and as he pressed just the right spot, the bricks swivelled just enough to allow him to slip around them and into a darkened room. Replacing the brick facade, he left behind the dusty and dank wine cellar and entered a cool room with a tomb-like silence. If there was any smell, it was the slight odour of paint and chemicals that greeted the nose. The lights revealed an immaculate, tastefully decorated apartment that could easily have been found overlooking the Champs des Mars in the seventh arrondissement of Paris, where in fact the furnishings had, until very recently, been found. He carefully hung up his spotless, white, double-breasted jacket and poured himself a tiny drink from a bottle on a mahogany side table, put on a favourite recording of Eric Satie, and settled into his customary Louis XVI armchair.

The TV reception wasn't the best, but given the location, what could one expect? The news report was crystal clear, though: a Christmas Day discovery by a Portuguese concierge named Maria at the Musée D'Orsay revealed that the Van Gogh masterpiece, *Bedroom in Arles*, had been altered, or more likely replaced by an almost identical copy, save for one crucial detail, which the police were not at liberty to discuss. The camera found a reporter with perfectly windswept hair holding a microphone in front of a stern-looking man in a bowler hat and suit.

"Inspector Magritte, all of Paris and art lovers around the world want to know what is happening to our treasured masterpieces. First the *Mona Lisa*, and now the Van Gogh bedroom. Do you have any clues?"

"*Merci*, Louise. It's too early to say, but never too soon for concern," he said mystifyingly.

The reporter nodded, pretending to understand, as Magritte continued. "An offence against artistic expression, whether it be an alteration to the *Mona*

Lisa or singing the 'Marseillaise' out of tune must not be taken lightly."

"*Mon Dieu*, they are even more stupid than I could have imagined," said the grey-haired man, peering in disbelief at his television.

"But Inspector, what methods of detection do the police have in these situations?"

Magritte appeared to be deep in thought as an awkward silence followed. "Louise, we must rise above the landscape of uncertainty and soar beyond the horizon of doubt on the wings of the possible."

"Good heavens, this is utter madness." The little man could no longer remain seated and fought back laughter as he stepped closer to the screen in disbelief.

Louise's bewildered expression was obvious and Magritte seemed to take pity on her. "Considering that Van Gogh used colours as feelings, perhaps we must apply an emotional logic to our investigation, *non*?"

Switching off his TV and downing the last drops of his drink, the man snorted, muttering to himself. "Fools. They look but they don't see. I must bring this closer to home for Monsieur Magritte."

Refreshing his drink, he made his way into a large workroom and flicked a switch that flooded the room with light, revealing canvases of various sizes on easels, all carefully draped with cloth. Everywhere were the artist's tools: brushes, palettes, sponges, glazes, knives, and varnish. He slipped on a smock and beret and removed the cloth from a small canvas. On a nearby easel sat a photograph of an almost identical work, both depicting an old pair of boots that strangely morphed into a pair of bare feet. The photo and the painting were stunningly alike, with one strange exception. He smiled at his handiwork, took a sip, and began humming a little tune as he picked up a brush and palette.

Seven

"That was a little too close," said Dizzy, pulling his cab out of the airport drop-off zone and heading back toward the city.

"Rudee's face looked like a hothouse tomato when he picked up the luggage," I said. "How much can Sashay's suitcase of scarves weigh?"

"Oh, I imagine Rudee is smuggling beets aboard. You can't see him going a whole week without the king of vegetables, can you?"

"No, I suppose not," I said, curling my nose at the memory of Rudee's pungent lunchtime favourite.

"Sooo," said Dizzy slowly, "I took the liberty of suggesting a day trip to Versailles for your parents tomorrow." I was immediately suspicious. "This just happens to coordinate nicely with the rally training session at CAFTA."

"Ah, so the Christmas festivities are over so soon," I said.

"I'm sure there will be lots of *buche de Noël* served with the hot cider tomorrow," said Dizzy with a smile.

The thought of those weighty chocolate logs made me sleepy and happy. "I love how they put the sugar on top to look like snow."

Dizzy glanced at me with a grin and I knew he was thinking what a child I was. So what, it was Christmas. Bring on the chocolate, whipped cream, and fizzy sodas!

The next morning, the parents headed to Versailles to discover the gaudy palace of the sun king, Louis XIV, while I went to a café in Montmartre to get together with a bunch of cabbies to learn as much as possible about road rallying in one go. Maurice and Henri Rocquette, the brothers who played in Rudee's band, The Hacks, were bringing things to order, never an easy task at the Café Taxi, where arm wrestling, card playing, and impromptu singing, sometimes all at once, were the norm.

"Attention, my fellow Parisiennes and winners of last year's taxi rally challenge…." Maurice paused, grinning, to allow the inevitable roar of approval. "Yes, we know the rules, the opponents, and what's at stake, but this year there will be new drivers and navigators."

At this point Henri jumped in. "And substituting for Rudee Daroo, who of course is on his honeymoon," here the drivers let out a collective *oooo*, "on a cruise ship in the Mediterranean," Henri paused dramatically to allow a group *ohhhh*, "is our favourite California girl, Mademoiselle Mac!"

The room erupted in a cheer, and I blushed. Is there any way to stop a blush? I think my mom imagines people in their underwear so she doesn't feel embarrassed. Yech! Maurice got down to business.

"For the drivers we've got new simulators to create the feeling of bumpy country roads in the south of France, and for the navigators detailed maps of the south and sample riddles to solve. *Allons-y, mes amis!*"

An instant din filled the room before Henri shouted, "One more thing. Madeleine has the new team shirts to hand out. What do you think?"

Madeleine, in her wheelchair at the front of the room, held up a shirt with the image of a grinning gargoyle, like the ones on the roof of the Notre Dame cathedral, at the wheel of a taxi. Cheers greeted her as she wove through the room.

Eight

"Leee-oooohhh." A gravelly voice that rattled dishes, woke sleeping pets in nearby towns, and terrified all who breathed, roared down the hall to a closed bedroom door. Behind the door a guitar was being gently strummed.

"*Oui, Maman*," a gentle voice replied.

"Come for breakfast now, and quit playing that infernal instrument or I'll use it for firewood."

"*Oui, Maman*."

A slender young man with a cascade of sandy brown curls falling over one eye emerged, barefoot with guitar, and sat down in the kitchen. "*Bonjour, Maman*." Leo smiled sleepily at his mother and put his guitar in his lap.

"It's a '*jour*,' yes, how '*bon*' it is I'm not sure," Margot Mallard grunted. She was a squat woman with thick legs, thick, tattooed arms, and no neck that was visible. What teeth remained didn't appear too happy about being left behind, and her forehead was deeply lined from a lifetime of scowling disapproval at all she surveyed. The lone exception was her son.

"Oh *Maman*, it's a beautiful morning. The rain sounds like distant bells, and the thought of a bowl of your porridge makes me glad to be alive."

"Ohhh, Leo." Margot shook her head slowly, but the roar had softened to a motherly growl, not without affection. "You're too sweet for the world, certainly for Marseille. But this year we're going to toughen you up, my little Ferdinand. You will be my navigator in the taxi rally and together we will honour the memory of your father by beating those five-course, cheese-nibbling, manicured, poodle-fancying, boot-licking dandies from Paris." As her voice built, spit flew and she punctuated this outburst by slamming her fist on the counter, causing the porridge to leap from the bowl.

"*Oui*, but *Maman*, I get so sleepy in the car."

"Noooo, Leoooh, you will not get sleepy this year."

"But *Maman*, I lose my way so easily."

"Noooo, Leoooh, you will not lose your way this year."

"But *Maman*, I have to practice for my show on New Year's Day."

"Noooo, Leoooh, you do not need to practice. You are ready now."

"But *Maman* —"

"No, Leo."

"But —"

"Lee. Oh."

"*D'accord, Maman.*"

She smiled and picked at her teeth while scratching her armpit with a hairbrush.

Leo asked shyly, "Would you like to hear my new song, *Maman*?"

"Of course, *mon petit*." Margot couldn't hide her pride.

Leo strummed and sang in a whispery voice with a sweet vibrato.

"*There's a lady known as Margot*
She comes from old Marseille
She'll take you where you want to go
As long as you can pay —"

Margot's eyes closed involuntarily and she rocked from side to side by the stove as Leo continued.

"*Margot drives her taxi*
So fast it makes you spin
Soon you'll see if you're like me
You'll be sorry you got in."

Margot's eyes popped open and she bellowed, "What!"

Leo leapt up from the table and raced down the hall with his guitar, laughing, while Margot chased him waving the hairbrush. He slammed and locked the door. "*Je t'aime, Maman.*"

Nine

"*She's a taxi girl/All she wants to do is grab a cab.*"

I reached across the pillow in the dark, knocking my brand new ultra-cool phone to the floor of the hotel room.

"*She's a taxi girl/Flag 'em down fast and jump in the back.*"

"Hello," I whispered under the pillow, expecting that Penelope had forgotten what time it was in Paris. On the other side of the room there was some restless movement.

"Mademoiselle, it's Bertrand the doorman."

"Uh-huh," I answered curtly.

"You have a visitor who asked me to call you on this number."

"Who is it?"

"He doesn't give a name," Bertrand paused, sounding sheepish. "Just to say it's a joke."

I smiled to myself. "Big guy, really big, looks like he could play Magwitch in *Great Expectations*?"

"*Oui, il est très grand....*" Bertrand replied, sounding nervous.

"Please tell him I'll be right down."

I left a note on the bathroom mirror, grabbed a banana from the fruit basket, and eased into the hotel hallway. What would Blag be doing at my hotel at four thirty in the morning?

"Hey Mac," he grunted when I spotted him pacing in the street beside his cab. I shrugged and waved at Bertrand, who retreated to the safety of the lobby. I gave Blag an awkward but sincere hug. Have you ever tried to hug a truck or a small office building? Blag was built like a low-lying mountain range, with a shaved head and a permanent five o'clock shadow to go with his gruff demeanour and intense gaze. I've seen people cross the street to avoid passing him on the sidewalk, and not just because he's a one-man crowd. What they don't know, and what took me a while to discover, is that underneath is one of the best people you'll ever meet. I would have been in a world of trouble — I mean more trouble — if Blag hadn't had my back during last summer's adventures. Oh, by the way, in French a *blague* is a joke, so you can understand the doorman's confusion.

"Blag, it's good to see you, but it would've been just as good if we'd waited until at least sunup."

"We have work to do," he said tersely, walking purposefully to the cab, "partner." He shot me as much of a smile as I would ever get from him, which wasn't much. I figured that part two of my rally training was about to begin.

"It's a lot easier getting around the city at this time of day," he said, handing me a grease-stained map of Paris and a few squares of paper with handwriting on them. "Okay, nana, you're the navigator, start navigating." He hit the sound system and an angry, siren-like guitar filled the car. As the thunderous drums kicked in, Blag began pounding the steering wheel and nodding in time to the music. A row of Viking action figures bounced on the dash along with the bass drum.

"What's the first clue say?" he shouted over the music as he tore away from the curb into the mercifully empty street. I shrank in my seat and held up the first piece of paper in the pile. It was written in an elegant, if spidery, hand. Blag read my mind.

"Yeah, Tawdry made up the clues. I couldn't think of any."

"Oh, cool," I said, "how is she? You guys looked great at the wedding, sorry you couldn't make it to the party."

"Yeah, well, I can only handle so much of the Daroo crew. And that carnival crap they play, ugh." Blag banged the dash in time to something called "Death Hurts." "Not like Malade, this is music."

I chose not to mention my dad's part in the music-making at the party. I flattened out the map on my lap as we sailed down Faubourg St. Honoré and read the first clue.

Like a belt it holds us in/This is where your day begins.

Blag chuckled as I stared at the map and thought out loud.

"A belt. A belt has notches and ... it goes through loops. Maybe it's an overpass.... No ... they don't have those in Paris, do they?"

"*Death hurts/It's a drag* ..."

Blag's singing wasn't helping.

"*But happiness/Makes me gag* ..."

I looked up as we approached rue Royale and caught a glimpse of the Madeleine church. What would Madeleine do in her little tower in Montmartre, from where she managed the world of Paris taxis with her giant map of the city? I closed my eyes, and there it was! The road that surrounded the city ... like a belt!

"It's the *périphérique*, Blag!"

"Nice work, short stuff, so how do we get there?"

Good question. "Okay, so let's stay on Saint-Honoré, right past the Palais Royale and head across the Pont Neuf."

"Sure, if it wasn't one-way the other way." Blag glanced over at me, grinning, and ran a yellow light.

I had to choose. "Rue de Rivoli," I suggested uncertainly.

"One way. Wrong way," he shouted as "Death Hurts" crescendoed.

"Okay, okay." I tried to keep my cool, already feeling over my head in my new role. "Then let's turn here up to Berger, past the Centre Pompidou, up to Francs Bourgeois, right on Turenne, left on St. Antoine, and around the Bastille."

"You got it, nav." Blag accelerated, thrusting me back into my seat, grateful for the empty pre-dawn streets.

I peered at the map but couldn't read it in the dim light, then I remembered that my new phone could be a flashlight. "Okay, I've got it," I shouted excitedly. "Stay on St. Antoine and circle Nation and take Cours de Vincennes all the way to the *périphérique* at Porte de Vincennes." This was one of the gates to the city that separated Paris from the suburbs on the other side of the *périphérique*. Relief was short-lived as Blag careened past a terrified vendor opening his newsstand, toward our first destination.

I unfolded the next clue.

See if you can find the star/The river means you've gone too far.

I didn't know where Johnny Depp's apartment was. "The star." Was there a telescope in Paris? I wondered.

Blag couldn't resist. "How's your French, kid?"

"Why?" I asked, "Oh, wait, star is *l'étoile* in French." I practically bounced in my seat. *L'étoile* is the name the locals give the Place Charles de Gaulle that circles the Arc de Triomphe. The streets radiate in all directions, making it look like a star from above. "Let's take the *périphérique*, now that we're here, all the way to avenue Victor Hugo, and then straight to L'étoile!" I celebrated by picking up one of Blag's Vikings and making it do a little dance on the dashboard.

"I'm Eric the Red and I'm going to L'étoile," I chirped happily, until Blag grabbed it and placed it, gently for him, back in its spot in an arrangement of brawny guys in capes and helmets.

"That's Leif Eriksson, Eric the Red's father. Don't you know anything important? What's next?"

Guess I was put in my place. I'd have to work on my barbarian studies. I read clue number three.

The little sparrow and Chopin/Know this is the place to land.

"Isn't there a bird sanctuary near the city?"

"Not sure sparrows need protection, kiddo," said Blag. "What do birds do?"

"Fly? Nest? Poop? Sing? Sing, that's it! My dad told me all about the little sparrow, Edith Piaf. And Chopin, it must be a musical reference, right? Like the *opéra,* or *cité de la musique.*"

Blag chuckled and turned up Malade. "Listen to this. Real music. Check this tune out, 'Obliterate Me,' it's their big ballad."

The speakers shook and I was having a hard time thinking.

"The Olympia Theatre. She made a record there. Did Chopin play there?"

Blag ignored me and headed into the sparse traffic at L'étoile. "Place to land"? The airport? Or the air salon, as Rudee called it.

"Hard to fly when you're dead," said Blag, "and there wasn't a lot of commercial flying going on when Chopin was rocking the Nocturnes."

I knew he was trying to help me, but I wasn't in the mood for sarcasm.

I looked at the map and noticed the big green patches, thinking that's where I would land if I were a bird. "Wait, the cemetery. That's land. Where is Chopin buried?"

"Père Lachaise," said Blag, catching my eye.

Père Lachaise was a vast cemetery that held the remains of some of the most celebrated artists, philosophers, and leaders in French history. "That has to be it. Edith Piaf is there. My dad said they leave flowers on the little sparrow's grave every day."

"Well, well, most of you Yankees figure the whole joint is dedicated to Jim Morrison of The Doors. Impressive. Okay, show me the way, kid."

The map was looking like spaghetti to me with the tangle of streets between L'étoile and the cemetery making my head spin. It didn't help that Blag treated driving a cab like a game of bumper cars. Oh wait — I scratched at the map. That was spaghetti. Nice.

"Okay, Blag, let's take Friedland to Haussmann then right at Place St. Augustine, around the Madeleine, past the Opéra. I can't read the street names, they've got sauce on them."

"No problem. Then what?"

"Then 4 septembre to Réaumur. What happened on September the fourth? Did Napoleon get his buttons polished?"

"Close. Nappy three got his butt handed to him by the Prussians so the third French Republic began. It was a big deal at the time, but, hey, let's just get to Père Lachaise, alright? Hint — stay on the boulevards, the small streets just mean that breakfast will come that much later."

"Right. Then rue du Temple, around République, and straight to Père Lachaise. We don't have to actually go in the graveyard, do we?"

"What? Of course we do. I'll take a picture on your fancy new phone of you on Jim Morrison's grave." Seeing my horrified expression, he added, "Kidding! Why don't you get busy with number four."

"Okay, it says *Where the wheels come to rest/and the bean juice is the best*.

"Bean juice? That sounds gross. Wait. Ohhhh, bean juice — coffee," I said triumphantly. "I know where that is. The wheels are on taxis, right?"

"You got it, Cal gal. I think Tawdry took pity on us and made the last one the easiest."

We pulled up to the locked gate at Père Lachaise. The sun was just starting to come up and it cast long shadows in the ancient graveyard. I shuddered and Blag laughed.

"It's actually a pretty awesome place." He could see that I wasn't convinced. "You know, if you like ghosts, zombies, the undead, that sort of thing."

I directed Blag up Menilmontant to Belleville to Villette and into Montmartre at the top of the hill. Blag's cab seemed to be on autopilot as he pulled up in front of CAFTA, one of the few places open at this hour.

I would find out later just how much Blag was not telling me about the rally, but what good would it have done to know in advance about terror on the country roads in the south of France? Of course, I also found out later that Blag had never actually driven in the taxi rally, or navigated for that matter, another small detail that he conveniently neglected to mention. Something to do with the fact that no one would get in a car with him. My stomach was just starting to settle after this morning's ride.

"Alright, nav, let's eat."

Ten

"Why do you bring the guitar, Leo? It looks like your girlfriend the way you caress it and keep it beside you all the time."

Margot cackled at her own hilarity.

"I'm an artiste, *Maman*," said Leo, lagging behind his mother as she puffed up the steeply angled street, leading away from their apartment in the Le Pannier district of Marseille, tucked in behind the old port. He took in the azure colour of the shutters, the elegant shape of the old street lamps, and the simple beauty of the laundry hanging between the buildings in the narrow alleyways as they passed.

"*Artiste*!" Margot spat in the gutter. "Is that what they call lazy daydreamers who sleep till noon with a guitar on the pillow beside them?"

"Hi, Leo." The daughter of the seafood shop

owner ran into the street and waved flirtatiously as they continued up the hill.

"Leo, will you play me a song?" a pretty waitress called from the doorway of a café with multi-coloured chairs on the sidewalk. Margot pretended not to notice when the girl blew Leo a kiss. She tried to pick up the pace but was now puffing furiously.

A girl in a raspberry beret passed on a bicycle with a basket of flowers. "See you tonight, Leo?" She tossed him a daisy, which he tucked into his lapel.

Margot held the railing with chest heaving as she arrived at her parking garage. "So, Leo, you have many fans in the neighbourhood, no?" When no answer came, she turned to see Leo far behind, patting a little black-and-white dog. She was exasperated with her son as always, but he managed to melt her heart nevertheless.

"Leee-oh, we have work to do!"

"*Oui, Maman.*"

When they arrived at the auto body shop, a cluster of white Marseille cabs lined the curb.

"Armand, *ça va?*" Margot called out to a reed-thin man in overalls with a wedge-shaped head and a tiny moustache.

"*Allo*, Margot, everyone is here." He held his breath during the obligatory air kissing. "I see you brought some entertainment." He flashed a yellowy grin and looked at Leo with amusement.

"This year we'll make a top-notch navigator out of my son," Margot said, "and a winner out of the Marauders."

A group of rough-looking men got up from a table at the rear of the shop, abandoning cider and food to greet Margot and Leo.

"Bravo, Margot."

"I like the sound of 'winner.'"

"Welcome, Leo."

"Leo, you remember Pépin, Baptiste, and Félix," Margot said as her son was greeted with back-slapping and crunchy handshakes. "He's my boy, but be tough with him."

"You can count on us," said Félix in a tone that suggested a rough ride for Leo.

"So, Margot," said Armand, getting everyone's attention, "this year I have brought in an expert to help us with our ... strategy." He grinned maliciously and the others nodded in agreement. "He's from Paris." A sarcastic "oooooh" followed this announcement. "But he was born nearby in the Bouches-du-Rhône, and believe me, his heart is with us. Meet Dr. Etienne Brouillard."

The lone straggler at the table in the back of the auto body shop stood up, wiping his mouth with his sleeve. He had jet-black, slicked-back hair, a quiz show host's tan, and a food-stained lab coat. Margot eyed Dr. Brouillard with suspicion as he passed his sleeve across his mouth again and flashed a gooey smile, with bits of ox tongue and gravy protruding from it.

"A doctor of what," she asked, "gluttony?"

"*Enchanté*, Madame Mallard," the doctor oozed. "I am a practitioner of mayhem, madness, and malevolence. If I understand my old friend Armand, this is what you require for the upcoming taxi auto rally, no?"

"*Oui, Monsieur le docteur,*" said Margot, "that is exactly what we need to show those Parisian milquetoasts who rules the road."

"Very good, Madame, then allow me to demonstrate some of my techniques for achieving that noble goal. Please, everyone have a seat."

As the drivers found their places, Leo sat on a pile of tires, strumming his guitar with his eyes closed. The doctor took this briefest of interludes to drain the plate of the sauce beneath the ox tongue.

"*Extraordinaire*, Armand. This is not the usual accompaniment to this exquisite dish, is it?"

"No," Armand replied, glancing around the auto body shop, "but we like things very greasy around here." This brought a round of snide laughter. "So we use poutine, a French Canadian specialty with fries, cheese curds, and gravy. If the ox still had his tongue, he would love it!"

The doctor laughed, belched into his hand, and ran it though his hair. "So, *mes amis*, to defeat the Partypoppers from Paris, a name whose origins escape me, an aggressive approach will be required. They are more resourceful than they at first appear and will be determined to defend their title." A general grumbling greeted this remark. "We must employ your detailed knowledge of the terrain, superior driving skills, and some completely illegal and totally nasty dirty tricks."

"Bravo," said Pépin, "the dirtier and nastier, the better."

The doctor pulled down a map of the route, which hadn't been released to any of the teams yet. The Maurauders were already impressed.

"Did I mention that their secret weapon is a fifteen-year-old girl from California?" At this Leo stopped strumming and looked up. The doctor continued, "How sad is that?"

The group laughed as one and the doctor gagged with amusement.

"We have our own secret weapon, Doctor," said Margot. "My son, Leo. He is a brilliant strategist and will be my navigator this year." She shot him her broken fence smile and Leo looked like he wanted to disappear.

"*Formidable*, Madame," said Dr. Brouillard patronizingly. "Alright, let's begin with some elementary evasive tactics, like sign swapping, fake roadblocks, and construction sites, and then move on to basic impersonation of officers of the law and emergency medical personnel. You'd be surprised how effective these simple manouevres can be."

"My sister-in-law is a meter maid," said Baptiste. "I could get some blank parking tickets from her." No one responded.

"Rrrright," said the doctor, "we'll finish with some easy-to-execute dangerous road conditions and the *coup de grâce*, the patented Etienne Brouillard disappearing foliage diversion."

The group sat silent, nodding reverently, clearly with no idea what the visiting mayhem expert was talking about. Armand went for a fresh round of cider, cigarettes were lit, and all eyes were on the doctor, except for Leo's. He strummed quietly on his guitar and sang to himself.

"There's a girl I want to know
All the way from California
When I look into her eyes
I'll tell her 'I adore you.'"

Eleven

I was inhaling the best *pain au chocolat* that had ever been baked while Blag hoovered up an eggy train-wreck-on-a-plate when my phone buzzed. Okay, you know it's the brand new ultra-cool one, etc.

Hey Mac, it's Rudee I'm on sail on the chip.

I assumed that meant "ship" and texted him back.

Hi Rudee how r u & Sashay?

We are waving.

This could mean many things. Was it auto correct or a Rudee-ism?

At CAFTA with Blag, he says hi.

Lying seemed so much more harmless in a text.

Are you a navy gator?

I thought about this for a minute. Navigator, it had to be.

Yes!!! Blag is a gr8 trainer!

Blag looked up from his breakfast.

"It's Rudee. He's on the cruise ship."

"Did he bring his own beets?"

"As a matter of fact …"

The food is for birds so I give it to them. I brought my own.

R u having fun?

We went to Pompous yesterday. Big fire place!

Pompeii. Cool!

Yes. And bowling and playing with the cruise control band while Sashay reads for tunes.

Fortunes, I figured. *K Rudee <3 to Sashay*

Be cart full at the rally Mac!

Yes, I'll be very cart full, I thought.

Twelve

My mom and dad were waiting on the curb outside the Costes, obviously stoked to be zooming around Paris. My mom had on a funky little *chapeau* and scarf set and my dad was humming a French song titled "La Mer" and snapping his fingers like a possessed lounge singer. Fortunately, the risk of running into anyone from my school was microscopically tiny.

"So, the Centre Pompidou has the George restaurant, which happens to have the most spectacular views of the city to go along with fabulous dining," my mom bubbled, guidebook in hand.

"And a wonderful collection of surrealist art, things you'll never see at the Louvre or the D'Orsay," said my dad.

Dizzy dropped us off near the museum. "And don't forget the Stravinsky Fountain, just beyond the square. A must-see!"

"Wow, it looks like they forgot to put the walls on the building," said my dad.

"That's modern architecture for you," said Dizzy.

"It reminds me of Bright Child," said my mom. "Remember, honey, when I took you to that baby gym and we'd slide down those big tubes together?"

I could see what she meant, and weirdly, it didn't seem like that long ago. Is that what happens when you're with your parents? Regression to childhood just a memory away? My mom took the escalator to the top floor and the breathtaking view while my dad and I went straight for the work of the surrealists like Miro, Dali, and Marcel Duchamp. Now, Marcel is a guy who submitted a toilet to an art exhibit and was surprised when he got turned down! You have to admire the nerve. He also did a version of the *Mona Lisa* with a moustache and a goatee. I wonder if her recent renovator was inspired by Marcel. My dad opted for the audio tour, which meant that he did a lot of unnecessary shouting, but at least I didn't have to worry about a repeat performance of "La Mer" at the museum. With parents, you never know what to expect.

It was here I fell in love with Magritte — René that is. The wacky Belgian with the raining men, the floating rock, and the guy in the raincoat and bowler hat with the apple in front of his face. Apple man kind of resembled the Magritte I knew. Wow! I could see where the inspector's personal style came from. My immediate favourite painting was called *The Red Model* and it was bizarre and delightful. A pair of shoes turned into a pair of bare feet and I just kept looking at it, wondering why I was so fascinated, when my dad approached and pulled off one headphone.

"So, you like Magritte?"

"I love him, especially this one." Then I realized where part of the fascination lay. The shoes, I mean the feet, were two left feet. When I pointed this out to my dad, he pulled off his other headphone and stared at the painting for a long time.

"What?" I said.

"Well," he said hesitantly, "unless my memory has completely left the planet, this is wrong."

"Wrong?"

"Very wrong. Magritte's painting is identical to this one, but has one left foot and one right."

We looked at each other with what I'm sure was the same thought. Without saying anything, we raced down the hall to the book and gift shop and hastily looked up the painting. There it was — *The Red Model* — two boots turning into two feet, one left and one right. We looked at each other in silence and then rushed back to the painting, where visitors were taking it in with the rest of the surrealist art as if nothing was amiss.

An hour later, the other Magritte, the living, breathing one, was doing that little steeple thing with his fingers, pursing his lips and nodding silently, while all around him people waited impatiently. The museum's visitors had all been escorted from the crime scene. *The Red Model* still had two left feet, and everyone in the small gathering of employees and security personnel wondered, in whispers, how long it had been that way and why no one had noticed. It wasn't long before our favourite reporter, sixties hair in place, swept down upon the scene, filled with breathless concern. She thrust a microphone in front of the inspector.

"Inspector Magritte, is this meant as a personal message to you, and by association the authorities, this newest art attack on the work of René Magritte?"

In a windowless underground apartment in the south of France, in the picturesque walled town of Saint-Paul de Vence, an immaculately dressed, grey-haired man took special pleasure in this moment.

Magritte paused, uncharacteristically, perhaps flustered. "Louise, I appreciate your concern, and of course that of your many viewers, as well as your deep interest in the artistic lifeblood of Paris." Louise seemed to be following Magritte so far. "But just as the great surrealist, no relation, would explore the realm of the subconscious, asking such questions as 'Where does the pillow end and the dream begin,' we can never know, with certainty, the true intention of any act, can we?"

Louise was not going to be diverted so easily today and dramatically tossed her hair back before continuing. "But don't you think that the choice of a Magritte to deface and the image of two left feet is perhaps a critique of the competence of those charged with solving these crimes?" Louise tried to look sincerely concerned, but she had the journalistic blade out at this point.

"Why yes, it just might be," cackled the little man, applauding the events unfolding on his TV screen, "don't let him off the hook, Mademoiselle Louise!"

For Magritte the philosophical smokescreen came so easily. "Like the mystery at the heart of Magritte's work, nothing is ultimately concealed." Louise's brow furrowed, and before she could think of a comeback, Magritte added, "I feel I must mention my gratitude to our young American friend who made this unfortunate but necessary discovery. Mademoiselle Mac?" He searched the room, spotting me before I could escape, and gently guided me in front of the camera.

"Mac, how did you know it was a forgery?" Louise asked earnestly.

"Umm, well, I didn't really," I said, looking toward my mom and dad, who beamed nervously. "It just seemed weird to me, I mean more weird than it's supposed to be. The two left feet that is."

"Are you a student of art?"

"Sort of. But is this art? Not the original, of course, but what's been done to it."

The smug expression on the little man, alone in his room, faded quickly and he muttered to himself, "Is it art? Who is she to ask? Is collage art? Is a toilet art?"

"I mean it's clever, obviously done by someone with the skill of an artist." I wasn't sure where my confidence was coming from. "But with the mind of a child."

"What?" shouted the forger himself to no one. "How would this teenager, from America of all places, have the slightest idea what I'm trying to say with my work?"

"It's pretty selfish to deprive the world of great art, just to make a joke," I said, on a roll now. "I wish whoever did this would grow a conscience and give Paris back its beautiful paintings." The room erupted in applause, completely surprising me.

"A joke?" the little man raged. "A joke? We'll see who laughs at my genius." He slammed down his drink, shaking with anger and shattering the glass.

"Well, Mademoiselle Mac, thanks for putting this latest insult to art in perspective," said Louise, relieved to wrap up.

Having received way more attention than I bargained for, needed, or felt I deserved from the staff at the Centre Pompidou, and of course my parents, I was glad to get out of the building. We had tried to check out the view that my mom raved about, but people kept wanting to take their picture with me. Dizzy had caught my act on the TV at CAFTA and was waiting for us at the Stravinsky Fountain — which is fantastic, by the way. We had an interesting family dinner at Alcazar in the sixth, revisiting the day's events and trying to connect them with the "art attacks" that had occurred since Christmas, which felt like it was a month ago. Come to think of it, this morning's training session with Blag felt like it had taken place in another lifetime.

Thirteen

I had a restless sleep with dreams that incorporated men in bowler hats with two left arms marching between the gravestones at Père Lachaise as I watched from the back of Blag's cab. I awoke with a shudder but soon was thinking of croissants and fizzy OJ, replacing my gloomy dream. I was about to tiptoe out of the room when I saw a fancy black envelope addressed in silver script to Mademoiselle Mac, personal and confidential. Almost alone in the breakfast room at the Costes, I opened it.

If you wish to unlock the mystery of the missing art, come to The Little Sparrow's grave at Père Lachaise at closing time. Alone.

"Hey, got a head start on us, did you?" said my dad, coming up to the table with a copy of the *Herald Tribune* under his arm. "There's a big story on the art attacks, as they're being called, and a little piece on the taxi rally I thought you might be interested in."

"Definitely," I said, sliding my plate over the letter. "What's on today?"

My mom arrived and kissed me airily on both cheeks. She was getting weirder by the day. "Well, your dad wants to drink coffee where a bunch of dead writers used to hang out. Fun, huh?"

He shrugged as if to say *you know me*. "Why don't we start with something we all like and then explore on our own. Your French is good enough to get by anywhere, right, Mac?" This told me that my dad wanted to commune with the ghosts of Ernest Hemingway and Jean-Paul Sartre on his own. I knew I could go shopping with my mom, but I also knew that she'd be trying to get me into little French girl blue-and-white boat neck sweaters. And that was not going to happen.

"Sounds like a plan," my mom said, "and the Eiffel Tower isn't far from the Bon Marché, I believe. Mac, maybe you'd like to see the Rodin museum on the way, unless you've had enough art for one visit."

"I actually want to check out the Christmas displays at the Printemps and the Lafayette again." I knew this would get the "See — she's still a kid" feelings going. Always good prep for doing something I knew I wasn't supposed to.

The Eiffel Tower visit took forever, waiting in line to go up and then a two-hour, five-course lunch-with-a-view. For me the coolest thing was the view of the Trocadero, the stunning horseshoe-shaped building with its multiple museums and gorgeous gardens. Far too many photos were taken, but freedom has its cost. I was checking the time nervously on my ultra-cool new phone, knowing that Père Lachaise closed at dusk. By the time I got off the Métro and approached the gates, the dusk had given way to darkness. There was an ancient gatekeeper sitting just inside; he was so still that I figured he was either sleeping or auditioning to be one of the full-time guests. He had a thick, woolly scarf wrapped around his neck and a lumpy fedora pulled low. The temperature had dropped and I wasn't prepared for it.

"Excuse me, Monsieur." I stepped inside the heavy iron gate. He looked up at me very slowly.

"*Oui*, mademoiselle." His voice was low and husky, but oddly refined sounding.

"I know it's closing time, but would it be possible for me to visit Edith Piaf's grave?" I pulled out a single bent rose that I had taken from the bouquet in our hotel room and tucked in my pocket many hours ago.

"Ah," he said quietly, "you have something for The Little Sparrow?"

"Yes, if I may. I won't stay long."

"Hmm, well why not, *pourquoi pas.*" He closed and locked the gate. "Follow me, *s'il vous plait*, you'll be our last visitor of the day."

"*Merci*, Monsieur." I was glad of his offer to escort me there. I had a map, but the cemetery was vast, with winding avenues of bare trees, dim streetlights and shadowy markers for the silent inhabitants of Père Lachaise.

"So, you are an admirer of Piaf's music?" My guide moved slowly and deliberately, not looking back.

"Yes, Monsieur. My dad is a musician and he plays 'La Vie en Rose' when he's feeling romantic." *What a stupid thing to say*, I thought.

We passed some odd looking monuments: a stone statue of a man lying on top of his tomb, his stone hat at his side, another of a man seemingly trying to climb out of his last resting place, and everywhere so many weeping angels.

"You have been brought up to appreciate artistic expression?" the old man asked, a strange sort of curiosity in his voice. He seemed to be moving even more slowly now as the wind clawed at my thin pink jean jacket. I pulled the tiny collar around my neck to fight the chill.

"I suppose," I answered, distracted by the deepening gloom as we wound through the dimly lit laneways of Père Lachaise. "Is it much further?"

"Not too far," he said with a distant tone as a dead branch went skipping by, startling me. "You see there, that's the grave of Modigliani. Do you admire his distorted women's faces?"

"I'm not familiar with his work," I said, feeling increasingly uncomfortable as the temperature seemed to suddenly drop a few more degrees.

"Yes, why would you be ... as an American." He turned and showed me an eerie smile in the yellowish lamplight. I shivered, and not just because of the cold. "Your accent gives you away, of course."

"Of course." I laughed nervously as he stopped and looked around as if to get his bearings. In the darkness it was hard to see the old man's face, with his bushy beard and hat pulled low. "Are we there yet?" I knew I sounded like a kid in the back seat on a family car trip.

I looked around at the gravestones, the inscriptions lost in shadow. He ignored my question and pointed at one of the nearby monuments. "Max Ernst. A German, but loved in France. The father of dada." I wanted to say "Isn't that the same as being the dada of father?" but thought better of it.

"Is that art?" Even in the dark, I could feel his eyes boring into mine, and I shook my head at what seemed like an odd question.

My voice sounded tiny. "I don't know, why?"

He turned abruptly and continued in silence, and I was regretting this entire outing. What was I thinking? I hated cemeteries. I had no idea who had sent that letter or why it had been sent to me. And I'd already seen as much of Père Lachaise as I needed to with Blag this morning. How I wished I had asked *him* to bring me here.

"There's your little sparrow ... Mademoiselle Mac."

My blood slowed. I was positive that I hadn't told him my name. I inched up to the grave, not looking back at my guide, and saw that it was covered in flowers, spilling over a stone cross that rested on the top of the tomb. I turned to tell the gatekeeper that I'd be all right and could find my own way out, which was a complete lie, but he was nowhere to be seen. I placed my sad little limp rose on Piaf's grave and noticed something odd. There was what looked like a newly dug grave with a tiny makeshift headstone and dirt piled to one side. My curiosity drew me closer and I had to pull out my phone flashlight to read the handwritten words.

The skill of an artist
The mind of a child

A chill that had nothing to do with December ran the length of my body. I slumped to the ground in terror. I was glad the caretaker was gone, but he was also my only link to humanity. A cat jumped off Piaf's grave, hungry for little sparrows no doubt, completing the Hallowe'en picture.

I knew I couldn't stay there. For one thing, I'd freeze, and for another the inscription scared the wits out of me. I started walking what I thought might be the way back when the first snowflakes fell. It never snows in Paris, I'd been told. Well, almost never. Soon I knew I was lost. I wandered, quickening my pace, till I heard voices and music. Three kids were gathered around a grave, smoking, playing guitars and singing something called "Riders on the Storm" that sounded like a song my dad might have listened to. They nodded when I approached but seemed uninterested and unconcerned. Clearly, I was the only one who thought hanging out in a snowy graveyard after closing time was strange.

I risked an interruption. "Do you guys know the way out?"

The two guys and one girl all pointed in different directions and then laughed. It was a teen remake of The Three Stooges.

"Maybe we should ask Jim," the girl suggested, indicating the gravestone belonging to, of course, Jim Morrison.

"Never mind, I'll find my own way." Somehow, just running into them made me feel less at risk. Then I remembered that Blag had called me yesterday and I would have his number in my phone. Naturally, he knew where Jim Morrison's grave was, or the Lizard King, as he referred to the singer, and he directed me to the exit, where he showed up minutes later. He pretended no surprise at seeing me there, but I'd caught his expression of worry as he was looking for me when he pulled up. How touching!

"Partying with the stiffs?" Blag smiled and opened the passenger door. I got in and held my hands in front of the heater.

"As a matter of fact ..." I let it trail off so I wouldn't have to start explaining. "Thanks for coming so fast."

"No problem, Cal gal. You got me out of checking out some folksinger friend of Tawdry's who had a gig in the Marais. That sensitive stuff makes me hurl. So where to, the Costes? What are you going to tell ma and pa you were up to, zombie chaser? By the way, I don't need to know."

"Is it possible to go by the Printemps and Galeries Lafayette on the way back?" Blag glanced over at me with a look of disbelief. "Thanks. And *joyeux Noël*, Blag."

Fourteen

Black and white posters of a man's silhouette popped up overnight all over Paris with the words WHO IS THIS MAN? in bold underneath. Sipping his café noisette in the first class compartment of the train for Nice, the small, neat, grey-haired man chuckled to himself as he read the account of the interview in *Le Devoir* with the headline ART ATTACKER SPEAKS. *That's the best they could do*, he thought while still thoroughly enjoying the grainy photo taken from a television screen that showed his noble features to excellent advantage. He tugged at his goatee and checked his reflection in the train window.

The previous night's TV special dominated both the airwaves and the city's conversation in the hours that followed. Star TV journalist Louise Lafontaine had been contacted secretly and offered an exclusive interview with the man behind the "art attacks" in exchange for a guarantee of his safety and anonymity. The drama of hearing the culprit's voice altered electronically and seeing his profile in silhouette added to the public's feverish obsession with the mystery. The outrage of the French public led to a chorus of voices demanding that Louise reveal her sources or be arrested herself. She claimed that her only contact was a very old, bearded man with a cane who arranged for the art attacker to arrive at the network by a back alley entrance at a precise time. Even the station employees saw only what the public saw, a silhouette, a shape of a face without features.

"Please tell us, Monsieur Réplique, as you have chosen to be called, what the purpose of these art attacks is."

Louise had gone all-out preparing for the biggest interview of her young career. Her nails glistened in a blushing rose, matched by her dewy lipstick and a dash of rouge. The tidal wave of auburn hair, her signature, was swept up, defying gravity and framed by dramatic backlighting. This was her moment.

"Very simply, Louise," he began in a kindly tone. "The art that we have all come to know and love and identify ourselves by has come, over time, to imprison our senses. We no longer see, we expect. We do not experience, we only reassure ourselves of our good taste. Our love of art is now at the level of our affection for a crisp white wine or a buttery croissant eaten on the way to work. As an aside, may I say that I do appreciate the odd sticky croissant *amande*," he chortled amiably.

"*Oui*, of course," Louise nodded agreeably, "and my day is quite incomplete without a *petit pain au chocolat* with my *café américain*." Here they seemed to be sharing a private joke as the nation watched, stupefied. "But Monsieur Réplique, even if we have become sedated by familiarity, does this work not belong to the people of France, and by extension, the world? What do you say to those who travel halfway around the world to lay eyes, just once perhaps, on a beloved Van Gogh, da Vinci, or Magritte?"

He could be heard sighing, as if having to explain something for the hundredth time to a child. "My dear Louise," he said patronizingly, "and may I direct my comments to those very people you refer to; have you ever stood in front of a Matisse, a Léger, or a Rembrandt, and just listened to the observations and comments of your fellow art lovers? Because I have, for many hours at a time, and frankly, these ardent admirers of creative genius and timeless beauty make me sick."

His tone turned dark as Louise seemed to sit up straighter, knowing she was getting to the real heart of the interview. The camera did a slow zoom in on the goateed silhouette. Snarkiness took over his voice.

"I love the colour of his hat, Bob. Couldn't he get a hotter chick than that to pose for him, Chip? No idea what kind of flower that is, do you know, Marge? When does the restaurant open?"

He stopped, and silence took over. You could almost hear Louise thinking of how to reply. "Sound familiar, Louise?"

She hesitated. "Well, I suppose, but surely there are some who ..."

"*Ah oui*," he interjected, tugging at his little beard like a beatnik Santa, "there are the art history majors who analyze the colour of the uniform of the twenty-second soldier from the left in the third row behind Napoleon to see if it suggests his childhood love of fire engines growing up in Corsica." His voice oozed disdain. "Let me be clear," he said condescendingly. "I am not a snob like the people who run our major art institutions," his voice curdled, "like the Louvre. If the works lived and breathed among us, I believe the people would appreciate it as their creators intended."

Louise came right back at him. "But even considering all this, do you, one man, have a right to alter the work of the masters to make your point?"

The French public held its breath, loving her challenging tone. The defiant flip of the auburn wave helped Louise make her point. But the little man came roaring back.

"I stand for those masters!" he thundered. "For they can no longer be heard. Their work should speak for them, but what it says is lost in the clamour of idiots with cell phones, mall dwellers, and café intellectuals alike with their collections of limited edition teddy bears, their trays of hundreds of shades of nail polish, and their smug little book clubs where no one gets past page thirty-five!"

Louise subtly placed her hands in her lap and

looked at the camera. "We'll be right back after these messages."

A break that included a gauzy ad for skin cream that would take decades off your face was followed by a commercial for a new mini "smarter than smart" car that could fit into a space the size of a fire hydrant, and a promo for a hot new daytime soap opera that revealed the petty jealousies and secret loves of a family-run cheese factory in Toulouse.

After the break, it was a flustered Louise who appeared alone on TV screens all over France. "I … uh … we … excuse me, I mean there's been a last minute change … a rather, uh … unexpected programming, uh … turn of events." The hiss of urgent voices could be heard in the background. "Monsieur Réplique, as he wished to be known, not his real name of course, disappeared from our studios during the break. I don't think he will return, since he left something behind. Perhaps he felt he had said all he needed, or maybe he feared for his safety, given the extremely controversial nature of his actions."

Someone off-camera handed Louise a black envelope with ornate silver script that read, *To be revealed only by Mlle Lafontaine to the people of France.* As she opened the envelope, Louise said, "I want you to know that we are seeing this for the first time and the network cannot be held responsible for its contents or the actions of its author." She seemed to be reading from a teleprompter. "It's called 'An Artifesto: Five principles by which we may learn to see again.'"

"1. Art must be 'with the people.' It cannot be the exclusive domain of airless mausoleums masquerading as museums. Witness the location of a beautiful Léger mural in the courtyard, or the Calder mobile poolside at La Colombe d'Or in Saint-Paul de Vence.

"2. Art must be 'about the people.' Is the beauty of a peasant woman kneading bread or the way a blanket drying on the line plays with the wind not as exquisite as so-called fine art?

"3. Art must be 'for the people.' Is the pompous prime minister who poses and pays for art the one for whom the greats should toil in order to afford their canvases and paint? Let the artist receive that fat government cheque each month.

"4. Art must be 'by the people.' Why not celebrate the creations of the seamstress, the florist, the weaver whose works beautify life very day?

"5. Art must be 'of the people.' Do we need another portrait of a pasty, preening, overfed secretary of state? Let us see the milkmaid, the delivery boy, the café waitress at work."

"These must be met or the so-called masterpieces will disappear forever!

Sincerely,

René Réplique"

Louise looked up from reading the "Artifesto" and simply stared at the camera.

A strange thing happened. It started with one letter to the editor of a small weekly paper in Brittany, in the north of France, and slowly gathered momentum. Some, not all of course, of what the art attacker said made sense to people. They were tired of not being able to afford access to the great works. Or if they did visit, fighting through a throng of shorts and sneakers-wearing loudmouths, arguing over whether Venus de Milo lost her arm in a tragic fencing accident or was born that way. The idea of art displayed in public appealed to a rebellious side of the French populace. One by one, major art institutions began an "*art à la maison*" movement with Monet and Caillebotte rubbing shoulders with pop star posters and calendars from the local *boulangerie*. Starting with the smaller museums, like the Jeu de Palme in Paris, the art of the people was given a viewing on Sundays. Even the tradition-bound Louvre, with Blaise Roquefort gagging and grinding his teeth all the way, agreed to an exhibition of finger painting by a particularly talented group of five-year-olds from a nearby school. The mysterious art attacker was triumphant.

Fifteen

It was not a festive gathering. The Partypoppers hunched over stale croissants, cold coffee, and mouldy cheese in a drafty corner of our Marseille hotel's restaurant. A spider dangled over the cracked sugar bowl, daring anyone to lift the lid, and tuneless music droned from a speaker above the door to the kitchen. Did I mention that it was six thirty in the morning, an hour I was seeing far too much of lately? No one spoke until Dizzy banged his fist on the table.

"Attention!" he said. "In one hour, we start the *rally de taxi* and we all need to be in the game."

"*Oui, oui*, but navigating on an empty stomach ..." Maurice trailed off with a classic Parisian shrug and a glance at the cheese tragedy.

"All night long I heard a dripping tap. Man, I sure could use a nap," Mink rhymed half-heartedly.

"My heat didn't work and the hotel said they were out of blankets," Henri moaned.

Blag sat with his eyes closed in silence; only his flaring nostrils told us he was still awake.

"And someone was playing the banjo above me at midnight," I said.

Maurice's eyes wandered around the room as Dizzy shot him a look of pure disgust.

"*Mes amis*," Dizzy said, quietly at first, pausing until he had everyone's attention. "We are the Parisians. We are the reigning champions of the taxi rally." His voice built in intensity as the group straightened in response. "Perhaps we should concede because there's something growing on our cheese today." He jabbed a knife into the ancient fromage and we all watched the handle wobble back and forth. The drivers smiled for the first time all morning.

"If we can't survive a dripping tap or a cold hotel room," he continued, waving his hands dramatically, "or a little midnight banjo concert," Maurice grinned sheepishly at me, "then how will we deal with the nastiness that is certain to be raining down upon us for the next two days?"

"*Oui, bien sûr*, you're right of course, Dizzy," said Maurice.

"Don't worry, we'll be there in fighting form," said Henri.

"Oh, and by the way, what would Rudee say?" Mink added.

"We are the Partypoppers!" Everyone chanted loudly, Blag perhaps a bit sarcastically.

"*Absolument*," said Dizzy. "I'll see you all in the parking area. Don't forget your team jerseys for the opening ceremony. We have to do Madeleine proud!"

Dawn squinted over the harbour, but Marseille was anything but sleepy this morning. A crisp chill in the salty air added a tang to the morning that made the nose twitch, and everywhere were the smells of fish and wet twine. Families clutching hot drinks moved quickly toward rue Paradis, the site of the rally launch. The teams, with three cars each, were pulling into their designated rows, separated by ropes and signs. The Champagne Supernovas, led by Anatole Belmondo, were all about style, their matching silver one-piece uniforms snapped like shrinkwrap into place on their svelte bodies. A bubble motif on their helmets completed the ensemble but led to some unfortunate jokes at their expense.

Next to them, the Bordeaux Bombes featured shapeless camouflage outfits, and the teammates as a whole looked like they would rather be elsewhere. The six Lestrade brothers, who looked nothing alike, whispered nervously and eyed the boisterous crowd with suspicion.

I don't know if it was a result of Dizzy's pep talk, the biting morning air, or the presence of the increasingly hostile crowd, but the Partypoppers were pumped by the time we got to our station. Blag had customized his T-shirt, cutting off the sleeves to reveal his new tattoo, a stylized T that became a woman's stiletto-heeled shoe, no doubt in honour of his girlfriend Tawdry. Maurice and Henri had slicked back their hair to look like it was soaked in motor oil, and Dizzy was sporting a variation on his usual pork pie hat. The *chapeau du jour* was gold with flames on the sides and only slightly ridiculous. Mink had aviator glasses and day-glo orange driving gloves, even though he was Dizzy's navigator. His rhyming had taken on a distinct hip-hop flavour.

"Hands on the wheel, you know I've got the touch, check it out baby while I double clutch."

I had my hair tied back purposefully, and Penelope's bracelet was polished to help me appear as threatening as I was ever going to get. I think the pink denim jacket may have undercut my menace.

The Marauders had yet to show up when a recording of the "Marseillaise" brought the crowd to its feet. Seagulls squawked along. As per the rally tradition, the Grandmaster, an ancient mariner in woolly navy garb, read the rules, which everyone except me knew well.

"*Mesdames et Messieurs,*" he said in a voice that sounded like it needed oiling, "and mademoiselle," he added drily with a nod in my direction, "four teams, three cars each, two days, and one glorious goal! To complete the journey from Marseille to Saint-Paul de Vence and back, arriving at each of the eight control points precisely every two hours, where the navigator will be presented with an envelope containing a clue that will lead them to their next destination."

The crowd, likely trying to stay warm, applauded this formality robustly.

"A reminder that all the rules of the Automobile Club de Marseille et Provence must be strictly followed in the interest of fairness, courtesy, and the dignity of the grand institution of driving a taxi cab in France."

The crowd roared with laughter and I thought that the Grandmaster smirked, but it could have been gas.

"There will be no diversions, no falsification of the route records, no obstruction of opponents of any kind, and no naughty words."

The audience howled.

"If we could have the captains of each team on the podium, please."

The Marauders chose this moment to make their grand entrance, horns blazing, the drumbeat from "We Will Rock You" blasting at deafening level and a team of dancers in sailor suits doing cartwheels alongside the Marauders' cabs. It was impressive, and the crowd loved it. A fishnet carpet was rolled out as Margot Mallard emerged from the lead taxi, a tank-like vehicle in freshly painted battleship grey with porthole illustrations on the doors. Margot shot a stream of spit through the considerable gap in her teeth and waved to the adoring crowd. She turned back and hissed something to the car's other occupant, who appeared reluctantly from the passenger side.

A boy of about fifteen or sixteen with what can only be described as a tousled look (Penelope, are you paying attention?) emerged in a blue- and white-striped shirt, red neckerchief, and yes … an eye patch! He slowly joined Margot, who grabbed his hand possessively and dragged him to the podium. *Her son? Must be. Cute? Might be. Lose the scarf and the eye patch and you'd really have something*, I thought.

The crowd chanted "Mar-got!" as she clumped up the steps to the stage. Anatole Belmondo couldn't hide his disgust, his nose curling at the sight of her; Marcel Lestrade couldn't hide his fear as he visibly recoiled. Dizzy took the high road, bowing his head slightly in deference and removing his hat. Margot scratched herself vigorously and then, to my surprise, looked down from the stage, pointed a yellowed finger at Blag and made the sign of the horns, which he cheerfully returned.

"You know her?" I asked, surprised.

"She's Margot Mallard, kiddo, everyone knows her in the taxicab world," he said with a tone of respect. "She'd force you off the road and throw you to the sharks before breakfast just for a laugh if you gave her the chance."

Charming, I thought, before asking as casually as I could, "So who's that with her?"

"The old guy? Oh, he's the grandmaster of the rally. It's an honorary position, whatever that's worth, and they choose someone different every year. I think he used to be the mayor, either that or a famous ex-con who owns a couple of shipyards, I can't remember."

"No, the younger one."

"No idea, why?"

"Oh, just curious, you know. He looks a little young to drive a cab."

"A little young for an eyepatch too, I'd say," muttered Blag.

Onstage, a barrel was wheeled out and the grandmaster announced that it was time to choose the lead taxi team. Belmondo rolled his eyes so dramatically you could hear them across the square. Lestrade sank into his camouflage and Dizzy smiled indulgently at the obvious farce taking place. A drum roll and a cymbal crash led to the grandmaster pulling a placard out of the barrel with MARAUDERS written boldly on it. The crowd went crazy as he held the sign up for them to see, revealing a fish hanging from a line that dangled below.

Margot leaned into the mike, cleared her throat of about a decade's worth of phlegm, and shouted, "Turbot powered!" referring to that favourite French fish. The "Mar-got" chant began again, and I noticed the boy backing away, preparing to disappear from the rear of the stage before she grabbed his sleeve.

"*Merci*, Marseille. We will not disappoint you, *mes amis*. Allow me to present to you my son Leo, my navigator *extraordinaire*!" Leo looked like he was wishing for an invisibility cloak.

The placards belonging to the Supernovas and the Bombes followed, and as expected, the Parisian team came last. We got in our cabs for the kickoff.

"Okay, kid, this is it," said Blag. "Got your maps?"

"I'm ready," I replied, but I didn't feel ready. I knew my mom's vision of the charming villages of the south and the blueberry picking wasn't realistic, but I was getting a feeling that the going was about to get very fierce very soon. I focused my attention on my well-read maps; I'd studied all the possibilities and concluded that since Saint-Paul was the first day's destination, we would likely not take the coast road toward Nice, since it would get us there far too soon. Everything pointed toward the A7, running north toward Aix, or some parallel route, but we still had to wait for the first clue. Right at that moment, the first envelope was handed to Margot Mallard and the gun went off, signalling the start of this year's taxi rally. To everyone's surprise, Margot swung her cab around on tiny rue Paradis, and instead of heading toward the autoroute, made for the harbour with the other two Maurauders cabs close behind. They soon disappeared from view.

"Where do you think they're going?" I asked Blag.

"Can't say, Mac, but you can bet that old sea hag knows something no one else does. They can't fix the clues — the taxi federation prepares those — but the Marauders will go for any edge they can get."

"Blag, look!" I pointed to the harbour, where a barge was easing out into the open water with three taxis on board.

"Perfect," said a disgusted Blag as he spotted Margot fishing from the side of the barge. The other members of her crew were tucking into their first beers of the day, and I noticed her son Leo sitting beside her with his hair hanging in his eyes, strumming a guitar. Did I say the word "cute" out loud or did I just think it?

"What are you smiling about, Yankee?"

"Nothing, nothing at all."

Our first clue was handed to me through the window and a flag was waved in front of us. Blag shot up Canebière, the old main street of Marseille, and a good point of departure in any direction.

"*The mane road goes not to the right, but to the home of starry night,*" I read aloud. Just as Blag came to a rolling stop at the first intersection, a stooped woman in a black shawl stepped right in front of our taxi. Blag stomped on the brake just in time to avoid flattening her. She swung around and gestured at him with her cane.

"Watch it, sunny Jim. You almost hit a defenceless old lady." She whacked the cane on the headlamp and stood glaring at Blag. I could feel precious time getting away.

"Haul it, granny, or I'll turn you into a hood ornament," shouted Blag.

"You mind your manners, young man. We fought the war for your sort."

Granny tried to kick the cab and lost her footing as a small but very angry crowd gathered. I leapt from the cab.

"Oh, I'm so sorry, Madame," I said in my most soothing tone. "My father is upset because ... his aunt is sick and ... he's rushing to her side to ..." I caught a look of incredulity on Blag's face, "... make her favourite dish for lunch ... cauliflower soufflé."

"Humph," she snorted as I took her arm and led her to the curb, "your papa has a soufflé for a brain."

"Okay, let's book it," I said to Blag, back in the car.

"Cauliflower soufflé?" he said, shaking his head.

"Best I could come up with. Let's focus on this clue. 'Starry night' must refer to the Van Gogh painting, right? But it's in the Musée D'Orsay in Paris, no?"

"Last time I checked," said Blag, bouncing a trash can off his fender and enjoying it a little too much, "but I'm having trouble keeping track of the art in the city these days." He looked contemplative, a rare moment. "But where did he paint it?"

I ran through my limited Van Gogh knowledge and the image of a chocolate on the pillow of the fake "bedroom" painting kept coming to mind. "Hey!" I said excitedly. "The bedroom is in Arles, right? And Arles is about an hour from here."

"Sounds good to me," said Blag. "Okay, let's hit the A7, this is easy."

"But we'd be there too soon."

"Not if granny had anything to do with it. What do you think? A Marauder dirty trickster?"

I hadn't thought of that. "Maybe, would they ..."

"With Margot, expect the worst and you won't be surprised."

"So the first part of the clue says, 'the mane road goes not to the right' and they spelled 'mane' wrong."

"There are no mistakes in the clues, Cal gal, so let's work it out."

"Mane could refer to someone with long hair. Joan of Arc before the bob."

"Or a horse's mane," said Blag.

"Yes! Where are the wild horses in the south?"

"The Camargue," said Blag, smiling, "just east of here and a longer way to Arles."

"Well, giddy up then, cowboy."

Blag didn't need any encouragement. With one hand he wheeled past the entrance to the A7 and with the other grabbed his radio mike and alerted Maurice, Henri, Mink, and Dizzy of the route. I explained our deciphering of the clue.

"Nicely done, little one," said Mink.

"It was mostly Blag, but we're a team."

"We are the Partypoppers," chanted the other drivers, and even Blag cracked a smile.

"I guess this explains the Marauders taking a barge. Is that allowed?"

"Doubt it, but the host team gets a lot of slack, probably so the judges don't get pelted with mackerel."

They sure figured out the clue quickly, I thought. *Leo?*

Dizzy and Maurice caught up with us in a few minutes and we proceeded caravan-style down the #568, what they called the *route ancienne*. It took us through small towns, the most picturesque aspect being the water, which came in and out of view as we rolled past. I kept a close watch on our route and the time, knowing that we had to be in Arles precisely two hours after our departure time.

About halfway, we passed through Fos-sur-Mer. The big highlight I recalled from my prep was the annual colour festival when all the people, streets, buildings, and dogs are decorated in the same colour. I believe this year it was aubergine, a purply French version of eggplant; they must have gone through a few shades to get there. Penelope would love this.

At the edge of town, the traffic was backed up for a funeral. A troop of sailors was carrying a coffin down the main street at a lead-footed pace. Blag wove around the knot of vehicles, which included frustrated members of the Supernovas and the Bombes, impatiently eyeing their watches. When we got to the front of the row, the pallbearers seemed to move even slower. I thought Blag was going to offer to carry the coffin himself when one of the sailors turned and pointed at us.

"Hey, mint-suckers, aren't you with the Partypoppers in the taxi rally?"

Blag shot me an "I knew it" look.

"Why don't you pull over? You can buy us all glasses of cognac and maybe clean our dusty boots with your minty-fresh Parisian tongues." At this suggestion, they all roared and the deceased shifted audibly.

Blag had heard enough and stormed out of the car to confront them, the numbers clearly not working in his favour.

"Ooo, in such poor taste for a Parisian to interrupt a sacred occasion."

The lid of the coffin popped open and another sailor sat up, grinning, and shouted "Death to the Partypoppers!" before the lot of them dispersed, laughing uproariously.

Sixteen

Rudee distractedly played solitaire shuffleboard, humming a gloomy little melody and gazing out to sea. A trio of gulls flapped and squawked on the railing. Sashay watched him from a distance, then came up from behind, wrapped a scarf around his shoulders, and kissed his yawning bald spot.

"You look like a man who has lost his beets," Sashay said sympathetically.

Rudee smiled feebly, "Oh no, *ma cherie*, my supply is ..." He stopped himself, flustered.

"It's alright, *mon mari*, I knew that you had a secret stash. I heard them rolling around in your suitcase. If you have any extras we could use them to scare away the seagulls."

Rudee looked hurt as he kissed her hand. "Mmm, you are well whiffed, my love."

"There was a sampling at the perfume bar on level

5. Heavenly," she said. "And I must remember the Hairspray Follies at three and Fingernail Fun at four."

"I'm glad you are polishing your day. I'm having a touch of barn illness."

"You mean cabin fever, Rudee?"

"*Peut-être, oui.* But I loved our visit to Sorrento. The eyesight was contagious."

Sashay let this one pass as a suave senior in navy garb waved jauntily. He wore a nametag that read Social Convener, Del Velure.

"Bonjournohhhhh. Ahhhh, there are my favourite turtledoves; I've been looking for you. Rudee, darling, the All Aboard Combo are delighted you'll be sitting in on organ tonight." Del cocked an eyebrow. "Oh, I hope I didn't ruin a little surprise for Mrs. Dovey."

"It's Sashay, and yes, the surprise is a bit mouldy now," said Rudee.

"Oopsy! Oh, and Roberto the band leader wanted to ask to which repertoire 'Stinkbomb Serenade' and 'Gateaux to Go' belong."

Rudee was mulling an explanation when Del added, "Oh, and Madame d'Or, your willingness to tutor the On Deck Dance Club in the romance of the scarves is so greatly appreciated. They'll be in Studio Swell in an hour, ready for you." He glanced down at his clipboard. "Oh my, I have to scoot scoot scoot. Bonjournohhhhh."

"Well, well, well, 'Studio Swell,'" said Rudee in a singsong voice that Mink would be proud of. But then something seemed to distract him and a dark expression took over.

Sashay put her arm on Rudee's shoulder. "What is it, *mon amour*?"

"I'm worried about Mac. It should be me pointing thumbs, changing the trunk, unwrapping clues."

Sashay pouted in reply.

"Don't misunderstand, my love. I only want to be with you, but little Mac ... you don't know those Marauders. They would curl the eyelashes on a crow."

Sashay eyed her new husband understandingly. "I know she's young, but Mac is very strong and resourceful. Have you sent her a message lately?"

"No, they must clam the cell phones during the rally."

"Why don't we go to the Internet café and try to get some news. The rally will have started by now."

A news report on Paris TV of course involved the ever-present Louise, and more speculation on the art thefts, since there was nothing concrete to report. She soon moved on.

"In other news, the Partypoppers from Paris got off to a less than stellar start on day one of the annual Rally de Taxi. I caught up, very briefly, with team leader François Caboche, or Dizzy as his road mates know him, while the team stopped in Arles at the end of the first stage.

"'Yes, Louise, it's been very challenging, but what do you expect when the best cab drivers in France go head to head or bumper to bumper? As always, there were some unexpected impediments.'"

"And how will the Partypoppers meet the challenge of, in particular, the team from Marseille?"

While she posed her question, a visual of the funeral procession in Fos-sur-Mer was followed by the sight of one of the Bombes taxis blowing all four tires simultaneously on what looked like a blanket of nails stretched across a dip in the road outside of Arles. The other cabs could be seen skirting the scene on a dusty shoulder of the road.

"Well, without giving away any squad secrets, let's just say that we have some highly specialized foreign intelligence that is helping to guide us to another victory!" At this the other Parisian drivers could be seen behind Dizzy, cheering lustily.

"Look, Sashay, there she is. It's Mac and Blag."

Sashay curled her nose at the sight of them covered in dust. "I hope they have bathing breaks."

"Of course, *ma cherie*, a long lavender bath and a pedal massage for everyone." Rudee laughed at his own absurdity, but obviously felt better having seen his friends. "Don't you have the silky seminar soon?"

"Ah, *oui*," Sashay replied, eyelashes batting furiously, "*allons-y*. Let's go."

Seventeen

The Bordeaux Bombes cabs were bunched together at one side of the control point in Arles, across from the arena, and strangely, a celebration was taking place. Glasses were clinking and laughter rang out among the six Lestrade brothers.

"Didn't they just get eliminated?" I asked my crew.

"*Oui*, when one of the cabs cannot reach the control point, the whole team is disqualified," said Dizzy.

"But why are they celebrating?"

"Margot," said Henri and Maurice at the same time.

"That cute bed of nails trick was just a sample of her handiwork," said Blag.

The two-minute warning was issued, so we headed back to our cars to await the next clue. I tore it open while we waited our turn to leave.

"Sur Le Pont we'll rest a spell, Ignore the 'I' but pick the 'L.'"

"Sur Le Pont d'Avignon."

I'd heard Blag sing before, and it was a brutal experience. His roaring metal favourites sounded like Pavarotti compared to this assault on the ears. He seemed to instantly regret it. "Okay, that's the next destination, but what's the rest of that nonsense about?"

I scoured the map for towns that began with an I or an L, but no luck. We were waiting for the other cabs to pull away from our checkpoint, the Arles arena, home to chariot races in the Roman era. It was a busy, touristy part of town with lots of cafés, and people continually tried to get into one of the row of cabs waiting for part two of the rally to begin. The Marauders, of course, drew first position again, and I watched as Margot pulled in front of the pack. Her son, Leo the navigator, kept looking behind them out the rear window, an odd tactic, I thought, until I realized that he was looking at me. He'd lost the eyepatch, I was glad to see, and he waved shyly at me. I saw Blag watching, so I didn't wave back. Leo held his hands up and made signs for I, L, and U before taking off.

"Hey kiddo, no time for daydreaming!" Blag was staring at me intensely.

Oops. "Sorry, I was thinking." I looked at the map, trying to understand the clue and Leo's intention.

"Well, I think I know what I L U means."

I blushed at Blag's sarcasm. "Blag!" I then shouted as the map made sense. "The route from Arles to Avignon makes an I, but if you make a U turn and go via Nimes, it makes an L!"

He didn't need to look at the map. When it was our turn, he wheeled around and wove through the crowd of tourists with the rest of the Parisians right behind. "Good work, Nana. I guess you really were thinking. Ha!"

We had drawn the number two position this time, with the Marauders in front of us and the Champagne Supernovas right behind. We all had the same idea, proceeding down rue de Refuge toward Nimes and eventually Avignon.

"Hey, Blag, why don't you sing the next part of the Avignon song for me." I smiled at him.

"Yeah, yeah. Very cute." But I could see him fighting back a laugh.

Eight roundabouts, seven sidewalk cafés, six dogs sleeping in the shade, five tiny cemeteries, four girls on bicycles with baguettes in their baskets, three French hens, two games of *boules*, and one Roman aqueduct later, we were there.

Eighteen

Quelle surprise. The Maurauders were still ahead and were positioned to lead off the third leg of the rally from the parking lot beside the Pont d'Avignon. The famous bridge extended out into the water but didn't actually go anywhere. I hoped it wasn't symbolic of our rally efforts. Seeing how easily the Bordeaux Bombes had been eliminated reminded me that every choice was important, so I pored over the newest clue.

If you find what marks the spot, try to get there on the dot.

It seemed so simple, but so elusive. Then it hit me. "X marks the spot" was the oldest clue in the book, dating back to pirate treasure maps, but in this case it referred to a place.

"Blag, I think X in this case refers to Aix, as in Aix-en-Provence!"

"Solid work, Yankee navigator," he said with a grin, "and 'on the dot' means that timing is essential, of course."

We high-fived, feeling very confident, and were exchanging favourite Rudee-isms when we hit a slowdown outside the Avignon city limits. Just ahead, a cop car with his lights flashing was blocking the right lane. A very tanned officer in rock star sunglasses and a handlebar moustache was standing in front of his car, and we watched as he waved Margot and her teammates through. He was chowing down on a local delicacy, the Boom Burger, as he held up a hand and stopped us when we got close. Something about him was familiar and weird at the same time.

"License and vehicle registration," he said through a mouthful. Blag handed him the papers wordlessly.

"This is a Parisian taxi. You need a supplemental permit to operate in Provence."

"We're on a rally, I'm not working as a taxi."

"Hmmm, and your passenger is in the front seat; that's a violation. And excuse me, mademoiselle, may I see that bracelet you're wearing."

What was it about him? I handed over Penelope's safety pin bracelet.

"She's my navigator, not a passenger," said Blag tensely.

"Well, monsieur, she's not driving, so here we call her a passenger." He smirked, and a bit of pickle that had been trapped in his moustache found its way onto his shirt.

"Here I call that ridiculous," said Blag, not hiding his impatience.

"Blag," I whispered, "he's looking for reasons to hold us up, let's not help him."

"Ridiculous, eh? Please wait in the car." The cop grinned at me with mustard between his teeth. He returned to his car with the papers. Many minutes later, with the time ticking by, he returned with another Boom Burger in hand and gave me back the bracelet, covered in grease. He looked at Blag. "Step out of the car, please."

Blag got out, fuming, and I was starting to worry about what he'd do if he lost his cool completely. He stood very close to the officer and covered him in shadow with his hulking frame.

The cop was busily writing up a ticket when he noticed something in our car. "What's that?" He pointed with his glove at the figures on the dashboard. Blag was confused and steaming. "Is that a Viking action figure?" Blag was speechless as I noticed a price tag on the officer's hat.

"Vikings are illegal in France." The cop put a glove in front of his face, belched, and seemed to stifle a laugh. "They're considered terrorists." Blag's lip began quivering as more precious time went by. "I'm afraid I'm going to have to confiscate Eric the Red." He reached for the figure and Blag snapped.

"Don't touch that barbarian, buddy. And it's Leif Eriksson."

I squinted and read the cop's badge as he leaned in the car: "Playtime Police."

"Stand back!" he shouted, and pulled out his gun. Blag froze as the cop emptied his water pistol on us, howling. He raced to his car, and as he drove off he tossed his moustache, with a chunk of tomato in it, on the road. As we pulled away, I spotted one of the Marauders' cars beside a roundabout with a pair of grizzled competitors collapsing in laughter when they saw us.

For the rest of the drive to Aix, Blag barely spoke. I knew he was concentrating on trying to make up the time we had lost, but the incident with the "Playtime Police" gnawed at him and I think he was contemplating revenge. On whom, I wasn't sure. I tried to cheer him up by playing his favourite music, Malade, Bloodjun, and the first album by Tonnage, the one before they sold out, as Blag had informed me, but he didn't so much as keep time on the steering wheel.

Nineteen

One by one, with the gentlest touch, he took the Matisse, the Miro, the Picasso, and the Léger down from the walls of the dining room of La Colombe d'Or. The tables were being rearranged and decorated to prepare for the *fête de taxi* taking place in the evening at the end of day one of the rally.

"*Merci*, Raoul," said Roux, the family proprietor of the legendary inn. "How was your little trip to Paris?"

"*Mon plaisir*, Monsieur Roux. It was brief but I believe I accomplished what I needed to. And I should be thanking you. It's an honour to be caring for one of the finest private collections of art in the country."

"The knowledge you've brought since coming here, as a former director of the Louvre, is incomparable. The family is grateful. By the way, did you see the interview with the 'art attack' thief? What a madman. You must find his actions despicable, as I do."

Raoul clenched his teeth silently and looked away from his patron. "I agree that his methods are ... unconventional, but I must admit to some sympathy with his thoughts on the appreciation of art."

"Hmmm, I suppose," said Roux, sounding dubious. "I was certainly surprised when he mentioned our little collection in such a glowing light. I still think he's a lunatic."

Raoul swallowed his reply and bent over to gently lift a Miro from the floor.

"I'm taking these pieces to the wine cellar where they'll be safe while I clean the frames and glass. With all the activity today I don't want to run the risk of an encounter with an errant broom handle or a slippery ladder while someone is replacing a bulb." He arched a brow knowingly and Roux nodded. He regarded the work with admiration. "I know this is a special night and there will be a room full of honoured guests and, of course, inevitably, the press covering the *rally de taxi*." As casually as possible, he added, "I understand they're a unique group this year, including an American teenager, or so they said on the news."

"Oh, I couldn't say," said Roux distractedly. "The preparations for tonight have taken all my time and attention. I hope it's worth it, given the unsavoury look of some of these competitors and their supporters. Speaking of them and the wine cellar, let's be sure the bar is well stocked. I think it will be a very busy place."

"No doubt." Raoul flashed a special smile for Matisse's elegant sketch of a woman as he carried her down the stone steps behind the bar. At the end of rows of bottles, he looked back to be certain he was alone before opening the brick facade into his secret apartment. He carefully eased the sketch in behind him and sealed the door, returning minutes later with an identical Matisse. Or nearly identical.

The road signs indicated that we were approaching Aix-en-Provence. It had been a slow, quiet two hours, but it looked like our timing was good, as long as nothing else got in the way. At the point where the highway gave way to the local road, there was a large detour sign, diverting us to the south and away from Aix. Blag slowed and looked over at me, obviously suspicious as a cab approached quickly from behind. Anatole Belmondo of the Supernovas raced past a hesitant Blag and blew us a kiss. The other two Champagne cabs followed closely behind as Dizzy and Maurice pulled in behind Blag.

We rounded the corner just in time to see the disaster unfolding. The Supernova taxis skidded into one another in slow motion like bumper cars and ended up in a messy cluster in the ditch, dented and disabled. A lone tire rolled away from the scene. An oozing oil slick glistened in the light and a layer of fog hovered above the road and drifted into the nearby woods. Five hundred metres earlier it had been completely clear. Belmondo wandered out of the fog with a stunned expression, his helmet with the bubbles dangling limply from his hand.

His bewildered teammates emerged behind him in obvious shock.

At that moment a breeze picked up and the fog partially lifted, revealing an odd character walking nonchalantly away from the scene with a device that resembled a giant leaf blower strapped to his back, wisps of fog coming from the mouth of the device. As he walked into the woods, he pushed a pair of protective goggles up onto his head and a slimy grin stretched across his well-tanned and now very familiar face.

We offered to give the Champagne Supernovas team a lift to the control point where they could arrange towing and decide how to get home. The rally was definitely over for them, and I felt a pang of guilt that a dirty trick, likely designed for the Partypoppers, had done in the unlucky Champagne team. We backed away from the oil slick and returned to the main road, where the detour sign was mysteriously gone and traffic flowed normally into Aix. Blag glanced at me, raised a unibrow, and slowly shook his head. He said one word: "Margot."

Twenty

At the control point it was a sad gathering of Supernovas who had been eliminated. No bubbly beverages were being popped today. The Partypoppers had a sombre look about them as well, given what they had just witnessed.

"I wanted to beat them, not destroy them," muttered Blag to me after we dropped off Anatole Belmondo and his navigator, "but the Marauders ... that's a different story."

Margot and her gang were laughing and celebrating like the rally was a done deal. A few of her nasty-looking crones broke into an impromptu performance of "We Are the Champions," a little prematurely, I thought. The only non-participant in the jollity was Leo, who sat on a rock in his own little world, playing his guitar and singing something so quietly, no one else could hear. My curiosity got the best of me and I walked over while Blag, Dizzy, Henri, Maurice, and Mink were angrily discussing the Marauders' tactics and fantasizing about revenge while waiting for the next leg to begin.

"And I'll tell her I adore you," Leo sang sweetly. He stopped suddenly when he heard me approaching, looking embarrassed.

"Hi," I said, "nice song."

"Oh, thanks," he said, "it's nothing, really."

"I'm Mac. I know you're Leo, I saw your mom introduce you."

"Hi Mac, nice to meet you. Yeah, that's my mom. The eyepatch was just a little embarrassing. You're from California, right?"

"Uh-huh."

"I've always wanted to go there. The beaches look amazing and I want to see a canyon."

"I live in a canyon, Upper Mandeville. You should visit some time." I immediately felt insecure, but Leo smiled and the feeling went away.

"*Oui*, that would be *incroyable*."

"Leeee-ohhhh!" A crusty voice that could wake the dead called out and Leo shrugged.

"My mother." He smiled conspiratorially.

"I figured."

"Mac, let's hit it, kiddo," Blag barked at me.

"Nice to meet you," I said. "I'd like to hear you play some more."

"Okay," he said, "as long as *ma mère* isn't around. She'd say I was conspiring with the enemy or something silly like that."

I laughed. "See you in Saint-Paul behind the battle lines."

Leo picked up his guitar and shook the curls out of his eyes. My heart did a little skip and I hoped I wasn't staring.

"Conspiring with the enemy, were you?" said Blag when I got back in the cab.

"No, more like infiltrating to learn their innermost secret strategies, Sgt. LeBoeuf."

Blag laughed. "Oh, so young Leo maps out their routes in his songs, does he?"

"Ha, ha, let's go, big boy."

The clue for the final leg of day one was about to be delivered. "This is the longest part," said Blag. "It's pretty much a straight shot, so I'm not expecting any of the usual Margot nonsense, but you never know. We'll have to really book it to stay close."

Flowered stones a tale to tell, walk and you'll be seeing well.

I had no idea what this could mean, and apparently neither did Blag. "Listen, let's just head for Saint-Paul. We already know that day one ends there, and you can work on the clue on the way, okay?"

"Sounds good," I replied.

Dizzy and Mink waved at us from Dizzy's trombone-mobile as they took the lead. Maurice and Henri followed, and we brought up the rear. As we headed for the highway and the final stage of day one of the rally, I thought of how much I had missed in the beautiful ancient cities of Aix and Avignon. The Roman architecture, or "architexture" as Rudee called it, the views from the surrounding hills, Picasso's chateau, the cool streets with their cafés and shops. I had to bring something back for Penelope! I'd been too absorbed in my maps and clues to appreciate any of it. The fate of the Bordeaux Bombes and the Champagne Supernovas was a cold reminder of what a serious business this rally was. At some point, when it was over, I was going to have to have a little chat with Dizzy to see exactly what he was thinking in selling this crazy event to my mom as some quaint tour of the charms of ye olde south of France. I guess Dizzy was desperate to find a navigator for Blag, who really was an excellent driver, and yes, maybe he figured I would do a good job. But then I recalled someone using the word "cutthroat" to describe the rally and I had to wonder. It was a blur right now, and I had navigator work to do.

I watched the French countryside roll by, the olive groves, cherry orchards, and vineyards. I found myself daydreaming of home. I love my home in the canyon with its butterflies and bougainvillea, the deer that visit at night and the lemon tree in the backyard. I wondered if Leo really would visit sometime. What was I thinking? I didn't even know him. And he was a Marauder!

"Hey nana, come back," said Blag teasingly. "Any ideas on that clue?"

The clue was completely baffling me. The first line seemed to contain the essence of it. "Flowered stones" — what could that mean? There were flowers and stones everywhere, although truthfully, about the only flowers in bloom this time of year were the yellow mimosas.

"Look, Blag, sheep!" I said excitedly. You didn't see that too often in southern California. "Better slow down, looks like a few are heading for the road."

"Stupid creatures," said Blag, slowing. "I'll go around them."

It was then I saw the shepherd at the rear of the flock, driving them toward the road and making it impassable.

"I don't know, Blag, they're on both sides of the road now."

He stopped the cab and slammed his fist on the steering wheel as the lamb parade continued. "We don't have time for this, kid, we'd better think of something."

The sheep kept coming, quickly filling the road behind us, meaning we couldn't back out of this situation either.

"See if you can find the moron responsible for this," said Blag angrily, "or I'm going to start making sweaters."

"Okay, hang on," I said. The flock was pressed against my door, so I climbed out the window. Not a shepherd in sight. I passed through the flock, now hardly able to see the outer edges of the mass of bodies. They were so innocent and gentle, I couldn't be mad at them, even though I knew that our rally chances were fading by the minute. We had to finish the first day within a certain time or we were out of contention. As a few pushed their woolly heads into my legs and baaaa'd, I spotted the shepherd, far away from the road. He appeared to be herding the sheep toward the car, and then I saw his tanned face and greasy grin. He waved at me across the bodies, a giant ham-filled croissant in his hand, and I knew we were sunk. The shepherd, the fake cop who'd pulled us over, and the man who created the oil slick that ended the Supernovas rally were all the same person, and it was someone I'd met on my last trip to France. Etienne Brouillard, the professional troublemaker who'd been part of a plot to destroy Paris's greatest monuments and turn the city of light into a city of darkness, was back and trying to help the Marauders win the rally!

Almost all of our remaining time was gone and we both knew it. Blag was morose and mostly silent on the road to Saint-Paul. There was no way we could make up the time and still qualify. We were still many miles away from the walled village of Saint-Paul de Vence when I saw a strange-looking character on the roadside ahead, standing in the middle of nowhere. He wore a long robe tied at the waist and carried a staff. A little old-school, I thought, but maybe this was the real shepherd. As we got closer, I could see how dishevelled he was, and just as we were about to pass, he lifted his hand as if he was flagging a taxi. To my surprise, Blag slammed on the brakes and pulled over onto the shoulder in a cloud of dust and gravel. Then he backed up.

"Might as well get a fare, make some dough, if we're out of this rally," he said, sounding resigned to our fate. It seemed like an odd choice, but it wasn't my cab. Even odder was our passenger.

"Bless you, fellow travellers," he said quietly.

"Bless you too," I said, sounding ridiculous to myself. Blag shot me a "who are you" look.

"Where to, buddy?"

"I go where the road meets the horizon," the man replied seriously.

"Great, that's where we're going too," muttered Blag. It was my turn to give him a "really?" look.

After an awkward silence, the stranger said, "You seek something that you believe is beyond your grasp." It wasn't a question.

"You got that right, daddio," said Blag with a snort of disgust.

I didn't want to be rude, but I couldn't resist a glance toward the back seat. The stranger had his eyes closed but he gave me a jolly thumbs-up. Weird.

"There is always another path." He sounded a bit weary, like he was tired of having to point this out to the uninformed.

"I wish there was another path to Saint-Paul de Vence," said Blag, "maybe one that involved flying or teleportation, whatever they call it."

Our passenger hummed to himself and seemed to be meditating when I looked back again. Blag shook his head skeptically.

"There is a moment, a fleeting one, which

is granted to us if we are open to it." *So Yoda*, I thought, *but somewhat entertaining and harmless.*

"When you pass the stone church on the right," our passenger said, sounding grave, "the sun will reflect off the steeple and reveal, for that one fleeting moment, *la route ancienne* in the woods behind the church. This, my fellow travellers, is your moment."

I have to admit to getting a chill listening to this little speech as Blag and I exchanged a "this is really getting weird" look. But then, right on cue, there was the stone church, and then the light reflecting off the steeple. The church bell chimed and an opening in the woods appeared where the trees had looked like solid green. It was about to disappear when I shouted, "Blag, now!"

I'm sure it was against his better judgement, but with nothing to lose — except maybe our lives — Blag swung the car hard to the right, bouncing off the shoulder of the road and landing on a narrow path that headed straight for a wall of trees. We'd missed the opening, I thought in terror, but it was too late.

"May the road rise with you," said our back-seat driver, sounding very chipper.

We barely touched down as we hit another rise in the road and became briefly airborne. I closed my eyes and thought about my mom and dad, in Paris, probably sipping a *coupe de Champagne* at the Hôtel Costes bar, hoping for a sighting of Johnny Depp, secure in the knowledge that their little girl was dreamily enjoying the simple pleasures of the idyllic south of France.

"Owww!" I'm not sure if Blag or I yelled louder as we landed in pitch black. It felt like the forest had sucked us into the trees that blurred past way faster than could be considered safe. I gripped my seat and clenched my teeth, and when I looked at Blag, he appeared frozen in place, his eyes transfixed on the way ahead. Our lights were off, the wind rushed past in a roar, and the path was a tunnel through the darkness. Blag made no attempt to slow down. Or steer. *This is not good*, I thought, but I knew it was too late to do anything but go along for the ride. We didn't speak.

When it started to feel like the road through the woods was endless, I saw a pinhole of light, rapidly growing larger. Seconds later, we flew out of the woods, like we'd been shot from a cannon into full blazing sunlight. Blag regained the wheel as we rolled bumpily past a tiny cemetery and through the stone gate to a beautiful walled village.

When we stopped rolling, Blag shut the car off and closed his eyes, breathing heavily. I had to get out and get my feet on solid ground. I stepped out onto an ancient stone street and looked down at the cobblestones, marvelling at their patterns of flowers. I looked back at Blag with a goofy grin on my face and saw that the back seat was empty.

Twenty-One

I was mega excited to share my discovery with Blag,
but he remained at the wheel, eyes closed. I looked
around us and saw the little cemetery we had just
passed, jutting out into the surrounding countryside.
I guess when a country is as old as France you've
got a lot of dead people to accommodate, but it
did seem that cemeteries were becoming a motif
on this journey. Soft clouds drifted overhead, a few
birds sang, and the hiss from the cab's overworked
engine slowly gave way to silence. We had rolled
to a stop just inside the gate to an ancient walled
village. Above the gate, set into the stone, was a
saint-like figure, looking not unlike our vanished
passenger. I spotted a pendant dangling on a chain
from the mirror that hadn't been there before. It
depicted an old man carrying a child across a river
and said, "St. Christopher."

"He's the patron saint of travellers," said Blag, breaking his silence, "or he was until he got demoted."

"Demoted? Isn't it a permanent position, you know, once a saint always a saint?"

"No, it's like the Brazilian soccer team that got moved to the second division. The fans cried 'bogus,' people rioted, but *c'est la vie*." This seemed like a bit of a stretch, but Blag was in a weakened state after our thrill ride through the forest.

"So that's who led us through the woods?" I know I sounded doubtful.

"I dunno, but I'm going to thank Chris anyway. I mean we're here, wherever here is."

I smiled as Blag blinked and looked around. "I think here is Saint-Paul de Vence." He looked stunned. "Check this out."

Blag slowly got out of the cab, steadying himself like he was on the deck of a ship.

I pointed to the patterns of flowers on the stone street. Blag slowly grinned. "I think you're right, kiddo," He looked at the town ahead of us, strangely quiet. "What's the rest of the clue say?"

"*Walk and you'll be seeing well*," I replied.

"Care to take in the sights of Saint-Paul?" he asked, and started up the hill, leaving our car parked at the town gate.

Saint-Paul defined quaint. It was one tiny street after another of charming shops, cafés, and houses with colourful laundry strung outside of second-floor windows. Rising voices greeted us as we rounded the corner past some civic buildings. In the centre of the town square a gathering of people of all ages surrounded a stone well.

"I guess we're 'seeing well,'" I said and Blag nodded, smiling as the crowd saw us approaching. They broke into a cheer.

"Partypoppers!"

We were draped with garlands of flowers, symbolic of our first-day victory in the rally. Amid the cheering, Blag whispered, "If you tell Tawdry I was wearing flowers around my neck, I'll be seriously unhappy."

"Your secret is safe with me, Monsieur Lafleur." I was more grateful for the hot cider and croissants that came with the flowers.

A whining engine drowned us out and a tank-like taxi rolled into the square, barely squeezing between the ancient buildings, scattering people and pigeons. Margot jumped out and stood, hands on hips, glaring at Blag. The crowd quieted like it was expecting to witness a duel. "High Noon at Saint-Paul" continued when I spotted Leo, still in the passenger seat. I suppressed a smile as he waved to me, looking more than a little amazed.

The two remaining Marauder cabs pulled in behind Margot just as Dizzy and Mink rolled up to the square from a narrow street on the other side of the well.

"Well, well, well, someone must know a magic spell," said Mink, obviously surprised but happy to see us.

Dizzy rushed up to me with a look of concern. "I was worried when we lost you. I guess I should have had more faith in your navigational skills, Mademoiselle Mac."

I shrugged, not ready to venture an explanation for our strange journey. "Thanks, Dizzy. I think we got lucky on this one."

Blag and Margot were still having an adult staring contest when Margot did that ridiculous gesture where you point at your own eyes, and then as if to say "I'm watching you" point at the other person. To my complete surprise, they both burst out laughing at the same moment. Margot's next gesture involved miming raising a glass, and Blag seemed more pleased with the prospect than I would have thought.

Twenty-Two

It was as if the vicious competition that is the *rally de taxi* was forgotten, or at least put aside for another day. Margot and Blag exchanged a burly bear hug and she appeared downright jovial as she shot a stream of tobacco juice between her teeth and onto the "flowered stones" of Saint-Paul de Vence. Leo emerged from their cab, looking as bewildered as I felt, grabbed his guitar from the back seat, and made his way toward me. If the Marauders needed an advantage, I thought, here it was. An artiste with curly brown hair and a shy smile. Dizzy, Mink, Maurice, and Henri warmly greeted their arch rivals, who it turned out were named Pépin, Baptiste, Félix, and Armand. Together with the locals and the rally fans from around the country we made quite a procession through the streets of town and down to the gate on the other side of Saint-Paul, where the other drivers must have arrived.

The sun had set on the beautiful hills of Provence. In the streetlight outside the Café de la Place, the old men played *boules*, which looked a bit like lawn bowling without the pins and without the lawn. On the other side of the square was an inn with a blue and yellow sign that read "La Colombe D'Or," with a painting of a golden dove flying over rolling blue hills. The words of my art teacher, Madame Ventighem, came back to me: "There is a small inn in the hills above Nice that houses a breathtaking collection of twentieth-century French art, given to the owner over the years in exchange for room and board." I recall she got quite misty-eyed at this point, saying, "And I only dream of going there someday." The rest of the class was, as I recall, given over to us attempting to create mosaics using little pieces of coloured paper that some of the boys treated like confetti, while Madame Ventighem looked dreamily out the window.

The terrace was filled with tables decked in white tablecloths and gleaming crystal, lit by candles. The wall separating the café from the town featured a dazzling ceramic mural of exotic women and a giant parrot, in golds and reds, tucked into the ivy.

"Léger," said Leo with a tone of respect, "a painter, sculptor, filmmaker."

The drivers headed straight for the tiny bar while the others sat where they could find a place, inside or out. I'd eaten enough pastry in town that dinner seemed unnecessary. Leo and I wandered into the dining room, which was more like an art gallery that served food. Miro, Matisse, Picasso; they all had a place on the walls.

In the bar, laughter, shouting, backslapping, and of course, wine drinking were in full swing. Leo and I tucked ourselves into an unoccupied window seat, seemingly invisible in the crowd. Henri and Félix of the Marauders were clinking glasses and discussing the differences between rallies of the past, like the Alpenfahrt in Austria and the Netherlands Tulip Rally.

"That Austrian nightmare has been going for over a century," said Henri.

"Much like yourself, you old toad," laughed Félix.

Maurice and Baptiste heatedly discussed driving techniques.

"I don't believe in double clutching," declared Baptiste, "it's for the ladies, present company excepted, of course." He glanced over uneasily at Margot, but she was engaged in an intense conversation with Blag.

"You're crazy," said Maurice. "The heel and toe technique is a noble and artistic means of changing gears." Baptiste rolled his eyes as Maurice continued, "Led Zeppelin drummer, the late John Bonham, used it to great effect in one of their signature songs, 'Good Times Bad Times,' no, Mink?"

"When you hit the kick, it's a Scandinavian flick," said Mink, coolly.

"*Mon Dieu*, what does a Swedish film have to do with it?" said Baptiste, waving to order another round.

In addition to a very busy waitress, the bartender was serving drinks rapid-fire. As I watched him go

about his work in the whirlwind of action around
him, he looked familiar, but I couldn't say why, just
something about his elegant expression, his reserved
manner in contrast to the craziness all around
him, and his hands, like those of an artist, with
long, slender fingers that gestured like a symphony
conductor.

Blag and Margot spotted us and Leo cowered.
"Uh-oh, here comes trouble, a lecture for sure, just
wait."

"Cavorting with the enemy, my little prince?"
growled Margot, but then she broke out one of her
ragged grins.

"I see you two are getting cozy," said Blag,
annoyingly. "Hey, you can settle something for us,
Monsieur guitar dude."

Leo looked suspicious and I couldn't imagine
what this was about.

"*Oui, mon fils,*" said Margot, "answer very
carefully. If Bloodjun and Tonnage were doing
a double bill at the Olympia, who would be the
headliner?"

Blag, from behind Margot's shoulders,
mouthed "Bloodjun" while Margot mimed carrying
something heavy, suggesting "Tonnage."

"Think carefully, little string man," said Blag.

"Navigate wisely, my little angel," said Margot.

"Well," said Leo hesitantly, "do you mean if the
concert was held today, or back in the mists of history,
when anyone cared about heavy metal music?"

"Hey, hold on," said Blag, and I giggled.

"And if being the headliner meant that the audience saved their most rotten tomatoes to throw at the stage…." I liked Leo better and better.

"Watch it, little wiseman," said Margot, sounding more than a little like Rudee at the moment. "Do you want to navigate from the trunk tomorrow?"

"Oh no, *Maman*, because we want to win, *n'est-ce pas*?" The rest of the drivers were starting to pay attention to the debate, and I could see money changing hands.

"Please remind me which band had a guitarist who played with his teeth."

Margot couldn't hide her excitement. "Tonnage, *bien sûr*, my sweet boy. That was Claude Hopper, the three-stringed madman."

"Well, then I think the headliner would be," Leo paused and the drivers leaned in to hear the result as Margot put her hairy arm over Leo's shoulders, "Bloodjun."

Margot looked stunned.

"Because no one should do that to a guitar."

"Yes!" exclaimed Blag, starting up a chant, taken up lustily by the Partypoppers, "Blood-jun. Blood-jun!"

In the noise I couldn't hear Leo, but he seemed to be justifying his choice to a stricken *maman*.

"Would you care for a beverage, mademoiselle?" A smooth voice spoke in my ear in the midst of the hilarity in the bar.

"But I'm only fifteen," I said.

He arched his eyebrow as if to say, "Yes, and it's a Tuesday."

"Orangina, *merci*."

I recognized the "it's your funeral" expression as he turned to Leo.

"Whatever mademoiselle is having."

The bar scene was soon too unruly, so Leo and I stepped outside on to the terrace. He strummed his guitar and I sipped my Orangina.

"So you can go to a bar at fifteen?" I asked.

"*Oui*, the laws are very relaxed, especially in the south," he answered. "I saw a toy poodle driving a Smart car just the other day."

Okay, for one brutal second he had me and knew it. He snorted some Orangina through his nose and onto his guitar.

"Serves you right." But I was laughing too. "So why did you choose Blag's band over your mom's? It seemed like it wouldn't matter much to you."

"You're right," he said, "but I had to get revenge for the eyepatch. I didn't want to do this rally thing anyway, but that was too much."

"Aarghhh matey," I said and Leo laughed. "So what's with the heavy metal showdown between your mom and Blag?"

"Oh, they became hard rock pals a few years ago. Legend has it that they were in the mosh pit at a Malade concert and my mom tried to climb on Blag's back to see better. He supposedly flipped her onto the stage, where she started dancing with the band, and I'm just so glad I wasn't there."

A giant raindrop splashed on Leo's guitar. It was followed by others. "Guess we better go in. That can't be good for a guitar."

"Oh, it's okay, it'll wash the Orangina off," he said.

The bar was even more crowded than before, so we hid under the eaves in a doorway at the back of the building. When it started to come down harder and began splashing back and soaking our clothing, I turned the doorknob and we stepped inside.

"What's this?" I asked Leo, as if he should know just because he's from France.

"Let's see."

We found a light switch and followed the steps down into a large wine cellar. The sound of the partying and the rain faded. "Wow, this is almost as impressive as the art collection." I said.

"Almost." He smiled and wandered off behind racks of dusty bottles. There wasn't much to see in the dim light, no vintage Orangina as far as I knew.

"Where are you?"

"Here." He strummed his guitar. It sounded cool in the basement, I mean wine cellar. I couldn't see Leo and it was getting darker the farther I went into the room. The boundaries of the room were invisible. It seemed to keep going and going.

"Do you take requests?" I asked.

"Maybe," he said.

"How about 'Light 'Em Up,'" I laughed in the darkness.

"Ha-ha," was his reply. I felt along the wall to get my bearings. There had to be another light switch somewhere.

"Whoa!" The bricks beneath my hand moved and a small opening appeared. "Leo, come here and check this out."

We squeezed through the opening into a totally posh underground apartment. "*Incroyable*!" he said, looking at the tastefully decorated, perfectly kept room. "If you could afford this stuff, why would you live underground?"

Leo put his guitar down by the door and we ventured in, not touching anything. It was all impeccable: the furniture, the light fixtures, the full bookshelf, right down to the decanter and tiny glasses on the table.

"Wow, this door is heavy," said Leo as he continued exploring. I was feeling weird about being in someone's place, fascinating as it was.

"Let's go back," I said.

"Not quite yet, Mac," said Leo in a strange voice, "not till you see this."

I looked behind me nervously and followed his voice. What I saw was astonishing. A vast artist's atelier with easels, paint, tools, and canvases. Once I could focus on the canvases, I was speechless. I felt a shiver run through my entire body. I looked at Leo and he just shook his head slowly in disbelief.

"Is this real?" I asked, but somehow knew the answer. There was the left foot/right foot version of the defaced Magritte, Van Gogh's *Bedroom in Arles*, without the complimentary chocolate on the pillow, and finally, in all her enigmatic glory, there she was, the crown jewel of the Louvre, the most famous painting in the world, the *Mona Lisa*, without her new wristwatch. We stood silently, in awe.

"She truly is magnificent, isn't she?" a genteel voice behind us said, almost sadly. "Without the crowds and their cell phones, making the same inane observations about her size, her smile, her true name ... she is indeed a masterpiece." He sighed deeply. "You know, I actually heard one visitor wonder out loud which Italian designer created her dress. 'Leonardo,' I answered, hoping to make her laugh. 'I don't know his line,' she replied, and I wanted to weep."

I recognized the bartender from La Colombe d'Or, but I also recognized him as someone else. He closed the door behind him and it sounded like the door of a plane when it's sealed shut for takeoff.

"Mademoiselle Mac, it's nice to see you ... again." Seeing my puzzlement, he continued in a low, husky tone, all the while eyeing me to get a reaction. "You have something for the little sparrow?" And then I knew. This was the same man who had pretended to be a guard at Père Lachaise. But who was he really?

Leo had been inching closer to me and I was grateful for his protective instinct. The man didn't seem the violent type, but his weirdness was very unsettling and I knew he wasn't happy with the two of us showing up in his private gallery of masterpieces. "You know this guy?" Leo asked, mystified by our exchange.

"Not by name," I said, "but by his bizarre and cowardly actions." The old man's lip curled in anger. "He wants to be thought of as an artist, but I suspect in his heart, when he is face to face with the real thing," I looked around the room at the stolen work, "he must admit, at least to himself, that he is a fraud."

"You know nothing," the man shouted, losing his carefully measured control, "and you know less than nothing about me."

Leo bolted for the door and had his hand on the doorknob, but the old man coolly picked up a remote and locked it without moving.

"Please," he said, "don't insult me. Just because we are in a room off of a wine cellar that no one knows exists doesn't mean that I would not take every precaution as far as security goes." He gestured across the room. "These are, after all, some of the gems of creativity of the western world, and it is because I respect and appreciate them that they are here."

He slipped the remote locking device into his pocket and strolled around the room, taking in the work like the connoisseur he was. "By the way, Mademoiselle Mac, I have no intention of harming you or your little paramour [I wasn't exactly sure what that meant, but I felt like I should have been embarrassed], but you will have to stay a while. When they come for you, and I assure you they will, you can be the one to tell the world about the work of the great Raoul DeFaux."

He lit a cigarette and settled into his *savour faire* man-about-town mode. I rolled my eyes at Leo, who looked both fascinated and disgusted by this whole affair. "You may not know this, but I, Raoul DeFaux, was the director of the world's most famous museum of art, the Louvre, until I was forced to retire over some petty issues of modernization." He gave a small shudder accompanied by the stinky upper lip expression. "What a shame that my successor, Blaise Roquefort, that snivelling little weasel, has had to endure this scandal so early in his time as director." Thinking back to my unexpected visit to the Louvre and encounter with the director, I actually agreed with the snivelling assessment. DeFaux made no attempt to hide his mirth at the effect of the scandal on Roquefort, and it occurred to me that revenge could underlie this whole business.

"Sadly, it may shorten his time in the position he coveted so nakedly and assumed so undeservedly by poisoning the minister of culture with lies about my work."

I felt like I could read Leo's mind. If we could play for time, maybe Defaux would slip up somehow, get distracted by his own genius, and we could escape.

"But how did you manage to create these ..." I had to choose my words carefully so as not to inflame the former director. I was going to say "fakes" but thought better of it. "... these replicas?"

He still winced at the term, but chose to indulge me. "I know everything about art," he said modestly, "not just who and when and where and whether they died penniless, or lived off of their mistresses, or whose faces they included in the background in exchange for financial considerations and protection from persecution ... I also know ... how." He paused briefly as if waiting like an impatient teacher for someone, anyone, to raise their hand. "I studied the classical techniques in school, but my work went unappreciated, so I grabbed the reins of power in the art world, all the while returning to my workshop at home, honing my skills, until now."

"But how did you do it, Monsieur DeFaux?" Leo's curiosity sounded so genuine, I think DeFaux was moved.

"Come here, young man, and learn." Leo approached DeFaux cautiously as he gestured at Mona Lisa. "My most challenging work, not because of the genius of da Vinci — that's easily replicated by a true craftsman — but because of age. I had to bake her many times in this oven," he gestured across his studio, "to achieve the exact *craquelure* that would have occurred naturally over five hundred years of heat and cold, expansion and contraction, leading to all the fine cracks you see in the older work." DeFaux suddenly swung around and glared at me. "Is this boring you, mademoiselle? I'm glad to have one young mind who doesn't spend his life with his eyes closed and his headphones on."

I told the truth. "No, it's fascinating. Weird, but fascinating." I was playing for time before DeFaux went all Hansel and Gretel on us with that oversized oven.

"Who could have foreseen," he thundered, "that it would be months before someone discovered the alteration to the world's best-known and best-loved work of art?" He allowed himself a small smile and, almost under his breath, added, "Of course, it could be attributed to the pure talent of the creator." I rolled my eyes, which did not escape the madman's attention. "And who would have imagined a child would be the one to see it?"

He suddenly sounded weary and defeated and sat down heavily on a stool in front of Mona. He took the remote lock from his pocket and mimed painting as if in a trance. Leo and I exchanged a look.

"Sad," said DeFaux in a hushed voice, "but it confirmed my hypothesis. We see not what we see, but what we expect to see, what we are told is in front of our eyes. People seek out the so-called 'important' works of art, the must-sees, and check them off like a grocery list that they can brag about at their coffee chain stores, their nail salons, and their self-important book clubs."

His voice sounded far away. Leo whispered to me, "What's this all about?"

"It goes with the territory. He's mad. He has to make speeches," I whispered back.

"Oh. You sound like you've had some experience with this sort of thing."

"Well, actually ..." But I thought a long explanation would have to wait.

DeFaux finally looked up. "So I raised the stakes. Van Gogh, Magritte, and now my boldest move:

to transform an entire collection of work without anyone noticing. Until I am gone, that is. Look. Appreciate."

He yanked away the cloths covering easel after easel of newly converted work. The prizes of the Colombe d'Or collection by Picabia, Matisse, Picasso, and Léger were all on display, or their close relatives were. Matisse's *Portrait of a Woman* with a tiny butterfly tattoo on her neck, Léger's vase with the tip of a cellphone behind the flowers, Picasso's round-faced man with a wisp of gelled hair poking out of his crown. DeFaux seemed to snap back to life as he gathered up his canvases.

"And I think I'll be needing my Italian friend as well," he said, while delicately rolling up Mona Lisa and easing her into the hollow of his cane.

"Is that how you managed to remove her from the Louvre?" I asked.

He responded with a superior smile.

"And as the museum director, you would have had unique access," said Leo, almost admiringly.

"Some diversions were required, but yes, I am probably the only person in the world who could have pulled this off. I know some things about the art of disguise as well." Here he pretended to be a much older man, giving me a chill as I recalled my experience with the gatekeeper at Père Lachaise.

"Where will you go?" I asked innocently.

DeFaux eyed me with suspicion, then shrugged. "I suppose there's no harm in telling you, is there? I have friends; more people than you might imagine are quite sympathetic to my work and have gladly offered their assistance. One of your rally taxi drivers, in fact, is taking me to Marseille, and from there I have secured a hideaway for the evening before an unscheduled night flight to Tahiti. Gaugin documented it beautifully, and I've always wanted to see it firsthand. As it happens, the extradition agreements with France are shaky at best, so I should be able to remain in this island paradise as a guest for some time. And besides, who will come after me, knowing that Mona could disappear forever should my safety be threatened in any way?"

"You would really destroy the most famous painting in the world to get what you want?" Leo sounded incredulous.

"I think he would," I said, disgusted. DeFaux offered only a reptilian smile in response.

"Ah, but I have a party awaiting me and I'm guessing that you two haven't heard. There's talk of cancelling the last day of the *rally de taxi*, or at least shortening it, due to the big storm. But you will be safe and far from all that here in my apartment. Feel free to use the TV and the fridge, but I would appreciate it if you would leave my Armagnac untouched. Sadly, I have no Orangina."

He didn't look sad as he made a swift exit, leaving Leo and I staring at each other, wondering *What now?*

Twenty-Three

Tireless rain flung itself on tiny Saint-Paul de Vence, along with the rest of Provence, turning roads into rivers, washing wildly over windows, and soaking every living thing that ventured out underneath the sky. Shopping, visiting, and games of *boules* were left for another day. Steady streams ran off the colourful tile roof of La Colombe d'Or and into the empty courtyard onto tables and between cracks in the concrete, sending wayward leaves rushing over soaked walkways, past bowing bushes in drenched winter gardens. Rain rolled into doorways, seeking any tiny opening. It dripped from trees and lampposts, drummed on car roofs, and danced in fountains.

Blag came into the bar of La Colombe d'Or and shook himself off like a bull terrier with a bad attitude. He looked at Dizzy and shook his head.

Dizzy peered out of a drenched window and heaved a mighty sigh.

"But where would she go?" he said. Around the table his fellow Partypoppers sat subdued and silent. Across the room the Marauders chewed on their coffee, playing a half-hearted game of Belotte. Margot looked up when Blag entered, a stormy expression on her face. Behind the bar, DeFaux fired up the espresso machine once more and turned to the grumpy patrons.

"Do you mean the American girl with the ponytail?" he asked innocently.

All eyes from the Partypoppers table swung towards him. "Mac," said Blag, "her name is Mac. What about her?"

DeFaux swallowed audibly and worked up a feeble smile. "*Oui*, Mac, of course. She was with the young man with the curly hair; I believe he was carrying a guitar."

Margot pushed her table aside, sending croissants airborne. "Leo. His name is Leo. What about him?"

She approached the bar alongside Blag, and DeFaux visibly trembled. With good reason. It was like having an angry brick wall walking toward you.

"Leo, *bien sûr*, Leo. Well, I saw them this morning, earlier, while I was setting up."

Margot and Blag, shoulder to shoulder, pressed against the bar as DeFaux shrank.

"They took one of the hotel umbrellas and headed into the street. Perhaps they were going up the hill to the magnificent Maeght gallery to view the splendid outdoor Miro sculpture garden." He shrugged.

Blag's eyes bore into DeFaux. "Are you sure?" he growled.

DeFaux's upper lip revealed a fine layer of sweat and quivered slightly.

"Sculpture?" spat Margot. "In a rainstorm?" Her eyes widened and her brow developed a furrow you could hide a roast chicken in. "With a rally to win?"

DeFaux's mouth smacked drily as he cleared his throat. "They were ... holding hands."

Blag's eyes closed momentarily and he shook his head slowly before turning back to the Partypoppers with an expression of bemused disgust. Margot snorted and shook.

"I'm going to turn my little Casanova's guitar into toothpicks for this."

A much-relieved DeFaux, with the focus off of him, let out a long breath and shrugged modestly.

At this moment, two local taxi rally officials entered the bar, drenched and shivering. DeFaux slithered over with a pair of espressos, which were gratefully accepted. Drivers on both teams eagerly awaited a rally update. A tall, pompous judge removed his raincoat and hat, downed his coffee, and cleared his throat.

"With all due respect for the time-honoured traditions of the taxi rally, it has been concluded by the local members of the Federation, after considerable deliberation ..." he paused dramatically, allowing time for the second official, a sharp-nosed young woman with a permanently arched brow, to interject.

"We decided over coffee."

A miffed expression accompanied the first judge's next pronouncement. "That this year's rally must, in light of the unforeseen, and may I stress, unfortunate meteorological conditions and their impact on the planned route …" He paused again.

"It's raining," his partner interjected, and when he showed his displeasure, added, "a lot."

"That the rally should be adjusted to embody but a single leg, reducing the final portion of this legendary event to its most practical configuration." He paused to allow time for full appreciation of his vocabulary, mistakenly, since the drivers seemed perplexed.

"You're going straight to Marseille, dudes," his partner jumped in.

The room exploded with questions, complaints, outrage, and confusion.

In the tiny apartment below the hotel, there was no evidence of rain, no talk of rallies or splendid outdoor sculpture.

"How long have we been here?" I yawned as I adjusted my position on DeFaux's tiny, perfect sofa one more time and looked over at Leo, who was strumming his guitar quietly with his hair hanging over the strings. *He really is very cute*, I thought as he looked up sleepily.

"No idea, Mac," he said. "Did you sleep at all?"

"Not really, you?"

"Not much. I guess we should reconsider the idea that we're going to be rescued from here."

"What's the alternative?" I asked, wandering over to look again in wonder at Van Gogh's *Bedroom in Arles*. "Do you think those are family members on the wall in his room?" Leo seemed to be deep in thought. "I wonder what he saw when he looked out the window." Still no response. "I wonder if *he* wore a watch." He looked like he was far away. I couldn't blame him; that was where I would have liked to be. "Hard to imagine Van Gogh with jewellery, even if they had invented ..."

Leo stood up suddenly. "What's that on your wrist?"

"Penelope, my best friend, thinks I'm stylistically challenged —"

"Yes, of course, but what is it?"

I ignored the "yes, of course" but might have replied a little sarcastically when I said, "In America we call it a bracelet, why?"

"Does it come apart?"

"Not if I want to still have a best friend when I get home, assuming we're not spending the rest of our natural lives in an apartment in a wine cellar."

"Let me see." He practically wrenched it off my wrist. "Sorry, I have an inspiration," he said. I figured it wasn't a new song idea. To my horror he rapidly undid the elaborate pattern of safety pins and began to straighten them out and bind them together into something weird ... that almost resembled ... a key!

"Nice work, Leo!" I said minutes later, so happy to be feeling my way in the darkness of the wine cellar once again. "Any chance you could put that back together once we take care of solving France's greatest art theft?"

"I don't think so." He smiled as we emerged blinking into the grey Provence morning.

It took me a minute to realize that it was far too quiet. There was no one around, no one in the hotel bar, no one in the street outside La Colombe d'Or. The rain had washed away everything in its path and the whole town looked soggy. Just outside the gate to the town, we saw one person, a mailman with an umbrella and huge rubber boots.

"They all went to the start of the rally in the square but probably ducked into the bars and cafés when it started pouring again."

"But what about the people from the hotel?" I asked.

He looked at his watch. "Siesta time, I think." He gave a small-town shrug. "Oh, except for the new man, the bartender who looks after the art." Leo and I were about to continue on into town but paused. "I saw him getting into a silver car with bubbles painted on the side. You don't see that every day in Saint-Paul."

We both must have looked mystified. "What direction did he go, did you notice?" I asked, trying to conceal the urgency in my voice.

"I'm a mailman, of course I noticed. They took the road toward Nice, not twenty minutes ago. Of course, you'd take the same route if you were going to Antibes or Juan-les-Pins, for that matter, or even Marseille, eventually. Now, there are alternatives where Marseille —"

"Thanks." Leo and I looked at each other and started back toward La Colombe d'Or.

"What are you two doing outside anyway? You'll catch your death." I guess every adult in the world is required at some point to say that to a kid who is willingly walking in the rain.

As we passed the Café de la Place, Leo spotted an ancient motorcycle with a sidecar parked outside. It was rusted and looked like it was held together with Scotch tape. Inside, the town gendarme sat at the bar with his head resting on his hands, snoring so loudly we could hear him in the square. The other patrons ignored him. Leo smiled devilishly at me and began to quietly roll the motorcycle away from the café. I looked back nervously as he said, "I think I've just figured out how we're going to track down DeFaux."

"Can you drive this thing?" I asked, not unreasonably.

"Maybe. But you're definitely the superior navigator," he said, handing me an equally ancient helmet from inside the sidecar that reminded me of my grandpa's football team pictures.

"This is going to play havoc with my hair," I said jokingly, putting on the bulky helmet.

"*Pas de problème*, Mac. You look *merveilleuse*!"

I like the sound of merveilleuse, I thought.

He kicked it into gear and the old bucket of bolts responded admirably. I looked back at the gendarme sleeping at the bar. He raised his head briefly but then went back to sleep as if this happened every day.

"I think we better head straight for Marseille," I shouted over the engine noise. "And I'm going to text Rudee so he can alert Inspector Magritte about DeFaux's plan." Leo nodded and we shot out of Saint-Paul de Vence toward Nice.

Twenty-Four

Rudee sat in the ship's lounge, nervously waiting for news of the taxi rally. "All I hear is flapping about the art surgeon and his manifarto," he grumbled to himself.

"And in other news," said Louise Lafontaine, the brightest media star in the country now thanks to her exclusive interview with the art attack perpetrator, "the annual taxi rally seems to be winding down in disappointing fashion for all concerned. Two teams were eliminated early due to some bizarre road conditions." Behind her the screen showed footage of the Champagne Supernovas walking away from the fog incident, looking stunned.

"Margot," muttered Rudee, "this has her footprints written all over it."

"Only the Partypoppers from Paris, last year's winners, and the Marauders, the host team from

Marseille who are heavily favoured to win, remain in the competition, which for the first time has been shortened to one single leg on the last day due to the heavy rains in the south." A shot of Margot and Blag eyeballing each other in a threatening manner came up on the screen as Louise continued. "In a final twist, two of the drivers, one from each team, will be competing solo after their navigators have gone missing." She then looked relieved to abandon this now very minor story. "But back once again to the major story we're following." She gave her mane a meaningful toss and returned to her beloved art attack saga.

Rudee sat transfixed in front of the ship's tiny TV, as if hoping he had misheard. "Mac!" The name burst from his lips as he jumped up and raced off in search of Sashay. He found her minutes later in a dance studio with a group of wannabe scarf dancers, all twirling awkwardly, some looking decidedly dizzy but clearly enjoying the lesson.

"Sashay," Rudee began, out of breath, "it's Mac, they say she is missing and the rain has shrunk the rally and I knew those Marauders would fog up the road and so we have to do something."

"Rudee, slow down, *mon amour*."

Sashay excused herself from class and led Rudee to the ship's deck, where he explained everything. At that moment a message appeared on his phone.

Rudee tell Magritte the art attacker has Mona going to Marseille.

"It's Mac," Rudee said excitedly. *R u k?* he replied.

Yes with Leo. Gotta go.

Rudee looked stunned and handed his phone to Sashay.

"Rudee, Mac says she's okay. Can you call Magritte?"

"We have to see the captain." He grabbed Sashay's hand and they raced toward the bridge. "I'm sorry, my love, but Monaco must hold itself. We have to go to Marseille, right away."

"Who's Leo?" said Sashay, but Rudee was flying past a group of wrinkled sunbathers on deck. In the captain's plush quarters, Rudee sputtered out a request to have the ship head for Marseille instead of Monaco because of Margot Mallard and her "dirty magic," as Rudee referred to it.

"Mr. Daru, if it was a medical emergency, we would go to the nearest port; and of course, we have doctors on board. But I just can't authorize a change of course of this sort for a ... what is it, a taxi rally?" The captain was offering his best "there, there" tone while trying to placate a severely agitated Rudee. "I'm sure the authorities have the art attack crime completely under control, and it's hard for me to see what diverting a cruise ship could possibly accomplish. I certainly can authorize you to use our phone to call your friend on the police force. Free of charge, of course." The captain directed a greasy corporate smile at Sashay. "And may I say, Madame d'Or, that your dance of the scarves at last night's show was charming and unforgettable."

Magritte was attentive as Rudee tried to engage his friend in the idea of a rescue mission, "*Oui*, Rudee, we have been completely immersed in this most obnoxious crime. There was a recent theft of canvas reported from a factory in Bourgogne that supplies a small but significant art school in Beaune, but it turned out to be a calculation issue with an inventory taken during the release of this year's Pouilly Fuisse wine, which from all accounts is shaping up to be a banner year for the wonderfully crisp white."

Rudee was as perplexed as ever by Magritte's ruminations. "But Magritte, Mac said Mona was going to Marseille."

"Hmmm," said Magritte, "perhaps a reference to 'Mona from Marseille,' one of the great French chanteur Maurice Chevalier's most romantic numbers. In fact, if I recall correctly, there was an outstanding version recorded live at the Olympia Theatre that I really must seek out for my next dinner soirée. Rudee, leave it with me, if you don't mind. I have to examine some graffiti on the underside of the Pont Neuf that could be germane to this nagging art attack business."

Rudee hung up, exasperated. "Sashay, this cannot be swept under the floorboards. We have to do something."

"But Rudee, why don't we just enjoy the last day of our honeymoon and let Magritte do what he does best?"

"You mean talk in squares and burrow his brow?" Rudee said, shaking. "Come with me, my darling, we have a rescue to operate."

Twenty-Five

Leo apparently did have a pretty good idea of how to drive an antique motorcycle, and despite the occasional bout of terror as we careened through small towns on the way or bounced over potholes left over from the Roman Empire, I actually found the whole thing thrilling. Leo's curls flew from the sides of his helmet and every once in a while he'd look over to be sure I was alright, flashing me that shy French smile I'd heard Penelope refer to. I had no idea how far ahead DeFaux and his collaborator were but I was pretty sure they wouldn't be taking the scenic route to Marseille. We had just passed through the town of Vidauban and the road was clear straight ahead, but then I spotted a gathering of familiar faces on the shoulder of the road. We zoomed by them and I took a quick look over as we passed. Blag! Dizzy! Margot! *Margot?*

I waved at Leo and got his attention, and he pulled onto the shoulder. We swung back and pulled up on the roadside. All six remaining rally cars were up to their mirrors in mud and were clearly going nowhere. Dizzy looked like he was seeing a ghost when I pulled off my ancient helmet and Margot almost seemed glad to see her wayward son. After a hasty welcome, they explained that they had been racing almost in tandem and simultaneously spotted a giant green apple in the centre of the road. I giggled but no one joined me. Apparently it was a big enough green apple that they had all been forced to brake suddenly and swerve to the right, into the sinkhole of mud. I mentioned the absence of the apple in question, but it seemed to be an article of faith among the six drivers. So I let it drop, reluctantly. Leo caught my eye and gave the smallest French purse of the lips.

"So how come you two went AWOL?" Blag sauntered over to me, covered in mud up to his shoulders.

"Did you try to haul the car out by yourself?" I asked teasingly. He shrugged and I knew that he had. "So, DeFaux ..." I could see that the name didn't register. "The bartender at La Colombe d'Or is the art attacker." He looked dumbfounded, and Dizzy, Mink, Maurice, Henri, and the Marauders gathered around to hear the story. "He's the guy who replaced all the art with replicas and he's got the real *Mona Lisa* and is planning to go to Tahiti, so Leo and I are racing to try to catch him before he gets away with it." As I sped through the story and watched their incredulous expressions, I realized how bizarre it sounded, but knew there wasn't time for a detailed explanation. I think they believed me, and of course Leo backed me up. Only Blag seemed to grasp the urgency of the situation. "Okay, kiddo, then you'd better book it for Marseille."

"Thanks, Blag. I'm sure the tow trucks will be here soon, and I'll meet you in Marseille. By the way, I texted Rudee to get in touch with Magritte, so help should be on the way."

Blag rolled his eyes and almost choked. "Yeah, those clowns are sure to save the day. Thank goodness Daru is on a ship in the Mediterranean and Magritte probably couldn't find his way out of Saint-Germain without a military escort and a trail of croissant crumbs."

DeFaux looked over at Anatole Belmondo, whose focus was intently on the road ahead. "I'm so glad you stopped at Le Colombe D'Or after the rally ended for your Supernovas team, Anatole. I'm not sure how I could have arranged such a speedy ride to Marseille."

Belmondo nodded but kept his eyes straight ahead. "You were the perfect host for my team, Monsieur DeFaux, and the fact that Dr. Brouillard made himself available to put the Champagne Supernovas back in the race made it a win for all of us."

DeFaux filed his nails and glanced back at Brouillard, who was tucking into the last bits of a suckling pig with zest. "So, Monsieur, or rather Docteur Brouillard, not to interrupt your little snack, but I'm very curious as to how you utilized my green apple painting — or shall we say my adaptation of Magritte's painting — to derail the taxi rally participants so effectively?"

"It was quite simple, Raoul. I projected your brilliant work onto a screen such as one would use at an outdoor film showing and turned it on once I saw the rally cars approaching." He proceeded to methodically lick each finger and the front of his shirt, where drippings from his "snack" had landed. "The massive size of the image, to say nothing of its content, was clearly confusing to the drivers. I'm no art expert, but the addition of a little bite in the apple was very tasty, so to speak."

At the wheel, Anatole Belmondo ran his hands through his hair and glanced appreciatively into the mirror. "This must surely be your dirtiest dirty trick, wouldn't you say, Brouillard?"

Brouillard cackled and examined his sleeve for any further leftovers. "Absolutely, *mon ami*. And I appreciate that you had no hard feelings after my fog diversion ended the Supernovas' rally. Of course, now, if you finish the race, you'll be declared the winner. I'd love to see the expression on Margot's face when she finds out how you pulled it off, but for the sake of my survival, I'll have to forgo that pleasure."

"So, Monsieur DeFaux, what made you choose the image of the green apple?" Anatole asked.

"Oh, please call me Raoul." He gestured suavely with his cigarette. "The Belgian surrealist painter, René Magritte, loved the image of the green apple, and in one work, mysteriously named *The Listening Room*, he used a giant apple the size of a room. It was my opportunity to remind Inspector Magritte of the Paris police how absurd his pursuit of me is."

Anatole only managed a fake laugh, but DeFaux seemed happy with the response as he puffed away with a self-satisfied expression. "Let me know when you're close to the harbour and I'll tell you where my boat is berthed, will you, Anatole?"

"Absolutely, Raoul. I think you're completely in the clear, so I'm going to slow down to the speed limit so as not to draw unwanted attention."

"Certainly, Anatole. I'm sure our swine-fancying scientist, Brouillard, took care of anyone who could be inclined to pursue us to the harbour in Marseille."

Twenty-Six

The slippery, rain-soaked pavement made the road to Marseille treacherous — as if being in the rusted sidecar of a beat-up motorcycle driven by an admittedly charming but totally inexperienced driver wasn't risky enough. I'd been happy to see Blag, Dizzy, and the boys, but their situation on the side of the road was no laughing matter, and the fact that Margot and the rest of the Marauders team were also waylaid made me realize that we had a common enemy. Could it be DeFaux or his associates, whoever they were? The mailman's description of the car that DeFaux took from Saint-Paul de Vence sounded like one belonging to the Supernovas, but was that lot capable of anything more dangerous than visiting a tanning salon?

I was getting used to the total discomfort of bouncing up and down in the sidecar, and my motion sickness problem seemed insignificant. Leo focused intently on the road, so I did the same. We passed every vehicle we approached, sometimes with very little room to spare. We pulled up on a very sleek-looking car with three passengers; the driver seemed to ignore our desire to pass. Then I noticed the bubbles painted on the side: the Champagne Supernovas logo!

Sure enough, Anatole Belmondo, the lead Supernovas driver, was at the wheel. He shot me a debonair smile, clearly not recognizing me in my 1950s running-back look. The passenger in the back seat was diving into a giant purple-coloured sausage that looked like it was trying to escape. He was hard to see but looked familiar and then, when he glanced over between bites, I recognized Dr. Etienne Brouillard, in spite of the rainy window and the bumpy road. He pointed at me and then I saw *him*. In the front seat was DeFaux! How these three clowns ever ended up in one car was chilling to contemplate.

Leo had been so focused on maintaining the road that he hadn't noticed the occupants of the car. Just then, Belmondo swerved dangerously close to the motorcycle and Leo had to move quickly to avoid a crash. He gave me a glance and I signalled for him to fall in behind the bubble-mobile. I mimed painting and he seemed to understand, so we hung back a bit but stayed close. What was their strategy? Then it was revealed as the Supernova car swung suddenly onto an exit toward the Marseille harbour.

The rain had started up again after a short layoff, and now, as we approached the harbour, a layer of fog settled over the entire area. Another trick? I didn't think so. It looked and felt like genuine maritime weather to me. The streets were narrow and bumpy, and more than once I bounced up in the air as we went over a broken patch of road. Belmondo's car handled all of this with ease, and despite the fact that Leo was on familiar turf, we couldn't keep up with them. The fog got woollier the closer we got to the water, and I thought we had lost them completely when I saw a hazy set of taillights in an alley to our right. Leo saw them too and spun around after driving past. We pulled into the alley in time to see Brouillard attaching a chain to a gate that blocked our way. He gave us a mock salute and hurried off into the dimness.

We abandoned the motorcycle, and although I was happy to see the last of it, I'd felt a little more protected with that armour of rusted metal. Now we were on our own in the silence of the harbour, with the sound of water lapping and the occasional distant voice echoing back from who knows where. Leo stayed close, and when we stopped to get our bearings, I could hear him breathing in little spurts. Was it possible that he was more nervous than me? Just then I heard the sound of boat bumpers rubbing against a dock very close at hand followed by a greasy chuckle that was all too familiar.

"*Merci*, Monsieur DeFaux, you've been very generous. Belmondo and I will leave you here. I'm assuming you can find your way to the Chateau d'If."

"Absolutely. Thank you both, I can take it from here. I'll be in international waters soon enough and beyond anyone's reach."

"If I see those kids, I'll take care of them for you. Call it a freebie."

"*Merci*, Brouillard," said DeFaux.

A third voice sounded a little less confident. "The waters around the island are treacherous, DeFaux," said Anatole Belmondo, "and I think we can forget about those kids. They're harmless and nowhere to be seen."

"Perhaps," replied DeFaux, "but that little Yankee agitator is relentless. I'm not worried about her doe-eyed suitor, but I'll be glad to see the last of her."

Safe for the moment behind the bow of a boat in the adjacent slip, I suppressed a laugh. Can you be terrified and amused at the same time? Belmondo and Brouillard, with his distinctive deep-fried odour, passed within a couple of feet of us as we huddled in the fog.

"I'll gladly take his money, and with it the chance to win the taxi rally, but this man is insane. You do realize that," Belmondo said quietly to Brouillard.

"Perhaps, but myself, I admire his trickery. The two left feet on the Magritte painting is a stroke of genius," Brouillard replied.

"Maybe, but those offshore currents he's heading into are wild."

As the two co-conspirators disappeared in the harbour fog, we heard a powerful speedboat engine kick in. Leo grabbed my hand and we raced down the dock toward the sound. Illuminated by the lights in the stern of the boat, we could make out DeFaux at the wheel by the silhouette of his goatee. He was moving out of the dock area at a dangerous speed, but I could see that he still had to pass by the end of the pier.

"If we run, we can get there as he's going by," I shouted.

We began to run toward the pier. "And do what when we get there?" yelled Leo over the engine roar.

"Jump!" was all I could get out as we raced to cut off DeFaux.

This was a race we couldn't win, as I could see as we neared the end of the dock. But I had to slow DeFaux down, thinking that even just a little bit might be enough to get us on board.

"You forgot Mona!" I shouted over the speedboat whine.

It was just enough, as DeFaux instinctively checked for the location of his hollowed-out cane and let up on the throttle. He didn't seem to see me and I realized that in the fog I was just a voice.

"Jump!" I yelled to Leo, letting go of his hand and going airborne across the oily waters of the harbour. I landed with a thump on something hard and grabbed for anything within reach. The stern light was mounted on a pole that was slippery and cold, but was solid enough for me to clutch onto and haul myself up. DeFaux had heard, or maybe felt my landing, and swung around at the wheel. The boat swung with him and he let up further on the throttle, likely to make sure he hadn't hit anything. Then he saw me, right as I heard a splash. Leo?

"Well, well, mademoiselle. I admit this is a surprise, but not a pleasant one," DeFaux called out. I steadied myself and started toward the front of the cabin.

"And while I admire your determination, I hope it is matched by your swimming skills." DeFaux turned back to the wheel and reached for the throttle. He turned the boat around and headed out of the dock area back toward open waters. I prayed that Leo was clear of the engine, but the smooth acceleration at least told me that we hadn't hit anything. I spotted DeFaux's cane, and thinking it could be my ticket to surviving this journey, lunged over a tarpaulin in the rear of the boat toward it. Right then DeFaux accelerated and I was tossed into the stern of the boat as the bow lifted in the water. I knew where the stern light was and held on like my life depended on it. Which it did.

He looked back and seemed surprised to find that I was still on board, if just barely. "Very well, Miss Mac, if you insist on being my passenger, *bon voyage*. But please understand that Mona and I are happy on our own in the captain's chair." He picked up his cane and thrust it toward me menacingly, and I backed up as far as I could without joining the marine life. But where was Leo?

"Rudee, I know you feel very protective toward Mac, but is this really necessary?"

Sashay wrapped her generous scarf tighter around her neck and shoulders and was grateful for its warmth as they bounced over the waves.

"I know she is strong like onions, but Sashay, my love, Mac is a child and her daddy and I spanked the road together," Rudee shouted over the lifeboat's engine as he peered into the gathering fog.

"You mean 'hit the road,' don't you, my darling?" said Sashay fondly.

"Of course, *ma cherie*. Did I tell you about the time we were doing a show at an archery range called The Crow and Sparrow and the target was on the bass drum?"

"Do you mean the bow and arrow, Rudee?" Sashay laughed in spite of her discomfort, as the wind picked up.

"As you wish, *ma belle*," said Rudee. "But when we forgot a song that had been requested, they took aim ..." Suddenly the engine stopped and the lifeboat settled in the water in silence. Sashay looked nervously at Rudee.

"One moment, *mon chou*," he said, and stared at the now-dead engine. "I'm certain I can make it quack like a bird, just a moment."

Rudee looked at the propeller with visible agitation. Sashay peered at the instrument panel and asked hesitantly, "So, Rudee, *mon canard*, when the little arrow is pointing at the 'E,' would that mean —"

Rudee grunted as he leaned over the engine dangerously close to going overboard. "One moment, *ma poule*, I will tell you about the arrow later…."

He paused, then raised his head and looked toward the bow with a sad look of realization. "You mean the gas tank 'E,' *mon ange*?"

Sashay just nodded and Rudee stared at the gauge, wishing for a different outcome. "I feel so fuelish, *ma petite*."

Sashay stroked Rudee's head where his comb-over had flopped to one side.

"Don't worry, *mon coeur*, we're not too far from Marseille, and maybe the wind will take us to shore," she said hopefully.

Rudee looked defeated, but then a slow smile took over his face. "The wind, *mon trésor*, did you say 'the wind'?"

"*Oui*, Rudee, but …" Sashay knew she should be nervous when Rudee had his look of inspiration, the most recent occasion having occurred mere hours ago and involved the theft of a lifeboat from their cruise ship.

"Unwrap your scarf, *mon coco*, and we will slide the wind, waving the mighty deep and sailing the sea salt…."

"Rudee, it's cold."

"*Oui, mon lapin*, but I will be the wind in your shoes." Rudee paused and looked seriously at Sashay. "Do you trust me, *mon mignon*?"

"Yes, I trust you, *mon loup*, but …" Sashay replied hesitantly.

"Then close your eyes," said Rudee, leading Sashay to the stern of the life raft.

"Alright, *mon minou*."

Rudee spread Sashay's scarf out to its fullest. "How do you feel, *ma poupée*?"

Sashay chose to ignore the fact that the lifeboat was standing still in the water.

"I feel like I'm flying!"

Through a space in the layers of fog I could see where DeFaux was taking us. A fortress of rock emerged from an island of stone. The fog gave it an otherworldly, sort of Hogswartian appearance. Is that an adjective? There was a grouping of rounded main structures, surrounded by stone walls with ramparts, presumably built to protect the inhabitants in an earlier era. It was hard to imagine anyone actually *wanting* to go there. But DeFaux wasn't anyone.

"So, little Yankee provocateur, what do you think of my island in the sea?" DeFaux turned to yell triumphantly. "As well as a fortress, it was also a prison holding The Count of Monte Cristo!"

"But that's a book and an imaginary character!"

"*Exactement*! That's why they cannot arrest me — it's a fictional location!" DeFaux seemed so pleased with his twisted logic that I knew there was no point in trying to reason with a lunatic. I just held on, hoping this journey would end soon.

The waves were growing in size and power. One hit the side of the boat and spun it suddenly to one side, spraying DeFaux and leaving me flapping like a drenched flag as I held on to the light pole.

"Even nature is on my side, child! No one will be able to reach us, and I'll be long gone in the morning when my Tahitian friends come for me. And for Mona!" He gestured with his cane wildly, as if he was conducting the storm. I was glad that da Vinci's creation was rolled tightly inside.

Another wave rocked the boat and drenched me in spray. "But Monsieur DeFaux, do you wish to spend your days on an island, even a beautiful one, far from everything that you love? Food, wine, Paris ... art?"

"Beauty is a moveable feast, little one. Ask Mona!" He cackled as he stood up to get a better look over the windshield.

The outline of the Chateau d'If was becoming clearer and closer, but so were the rocks that surrounded the island and threatened to tear our boat to bits. We ran up the side of a huge wave and came crashing down the other side. I was thrown forward and landed on the tarpaulin when I felt something moving underneath. My heart stopped. DeFaux yanked the throttle to its fullest and I began to slide toward the water when a hand reached up from under the tarp and grasped my arm. Leo! His smiling face looked up at me from beneath the covering. I was certain that DeFaux had no idea his boat carried a third passenger. Or fourth, if you counted Mona Lisa. Then I saw my opportunity: with what remained of Penelope's bracelet I reached toward the stern and sliced the fuel line while Leo held on and kept me from going overboard. As we bounced over the waves, I flopped like a sleepless salmon, until suddenly the boat came to a halt. DeFaux looked around, mystified, and shouted something at me, but the sound of a helicopter drowned him out. I couldn't see it but knew it must be just above us.

DeFaux now looked confused and angry, but not out of resources. He grabbed a paddle from the side of the boat and started working his way between the rocks that jutted out of the water and toward the harbour, which had appeared on the coast of the island. We weren't bouncing as wildly now that we were almost into the harbour, and I felt Leo let go and then saw him slip into the icy waters. DeFaux was paddling furiously when a voice boomed out of the fog.

"Give up, Monsieur DeFaux, there's nowhere to go!" Magritte! The inspector became visible, hanging on to a ladder that was being lowered from the helicopter hovering above us. He had his bowler hat and raincoat on and was carrying an umbrella, of course. I mean, you never know with the weather here, right?

DeFaux stopped paddling and looked up. He held his paddle aloft like he was going to swat away anything that approached from above. "Magritte, you bumbling fool, don't you realize I have a hostage?"

He began paddling again and was making good progress toward the harbour. Who knew what might protect him once he got there, or even if anyone could land. I crawled toward the bow of the boat as it bounced on the waves in and around the rocky shoreline. Suddenly, DeFaux looked like he was being pulled into the water. Then I saw Leo's head emerge and yank the paddle from DeFaux's grasp. DeFaux looked stunned but quickly swung around and grabbed his cane. Magritte called out to him.

"DeFaux, she's done you no harm. Except perhaps for some rather ill-considered comments during an impromptu TV interview that may have besmirched your reputation slightly, but which arguably are not entirely ..."

DeFaux yelled back, sounding exasperated, "Magritte, you raging windbag, what do I care about a child whose idea of art is taking pictures of herself on a portable phone? No, my hostage is far more valuable." He unrolled Mona Lisa from inside the shaft of his cane and held her up in the air.

"Monsieur DeFaux — may I call you Raoul? — ignoring for the moment your rather callous mischaracterization of myself, in the name of all that is sacred to art lovers, please put this most glittering gem of Renaissance genius back inside your cane." This was the most agitated I'd ever heard Magritte sound as he called out urgently through a megaphone from his perch on the ladder above the boat. "I have spoken with the minister of culture and he has agreed to arrange for an exhibit of your work at the Grand Palais in the spring. You can be completely involved in the mounting of the exhibition —

of course, from the confines of a comfortably appointed prison apartment with the highest quality furnishings, a superior thread count on the bedding, and a generous supply of fine liquor."

DeFaux seemed to hesitate at this suggestion but then threw his head back, laughing like a cartoon villain. "A most excellent attempt, Magritte, I must give you credit. But I know that will never happen, because I'm not going to prison. I'm going to follow my beautiful Mona to the bottom of the Mediterranean."

At that moment, he cocked his arm back with Mona in hand and flung the world's most famous painting into the air, destined for a home in the ocean. Magritte froze. Everything seemed to slip into slow motion.

"Noooo!" I shouted, as if that would slow down *La Joconde*'s progress into becoming only a memory. I threw off my sneakers, climbed up on the gunwale of the speedboat, and, checking hastily for looming rocks, I dove. I can swim, barely, but sometimes you have to forget that you might not be able to do something, not even giving fear time to form in your head, and just find that single purpose that hopefully will get you through the stupidest thing you could possibly do, given the circumstances. "Aaaaahhhhh," I shouted when I hit the water, so cold I thought my head would explode. Then I saw her, caught in a momentary, blessed crosswind, held up for her last public viewing before entering an afterlife with the fishes. I pushed forward through an advancing wave and threw my hand upwards underneath her. I kept my hand aloft even as my arm ached with the effort until through the ocean spray I saw a ladder lowering rapidly and a hand reach down to take her from me. An arm wrapped itself around me and the rest becomes a bit blurry.

"I feel like I'm flying."

I knew that voice! I looked up groggily and realized I was wrapped in tarpaulin on the deck of DeFaux's boat. The crazy genius was nowhere to be seen, but Leo looked down at me with great concern. Magritte was still standing on the ladder hanging from the helicopter, admiring Mona Lisa with a magnifying glass, nodding contentedly. Just then another craft emerged from out of the fog, some kind of inflatable rescue boat with a bizarre paisley-patterned sail.

"Little Mac!"

I definitely knew that voice!

"For flying out cloud, are you alright?"

I waved at Rudee to let him know I was okay and then realized that it was Sashay's scarf that was the sail. She was standing, arms outstretched *Titanic*-like at the bow, smiling at me.

"Leeeeeeoooohhhh!" A bellowing foghorn voice cut through the mist and Margot Mallard emerged, standing at the front of a slow-moving barge. "Where's my beautiful boy?" she called out, sounding stricken.

"Right here, *Maman*," Leo answered. Then I saw Blag at the rear, navigating the barge through the fog, which was starting to lift slightly. He grinned at me, and I'd never seen him look so happy.

"Nice work, shortie. I knew you could roll with the punches."

I waved at him and he gave me a thumbs-up. "Where's that goat-bearded nutcase gotten to?"

"He dove into the water right after he threw the painting," said Leo.

"Don't worry about him," I said, "Is Mona okay?"

"High and dry. Hey, Rudee," called Blag, "have you got an inner tube on that rig?"

"Sure, Blag," said Rudee, grinning, "with a long rope for some ocean rodeo!"

"Cool," said Blag. "Why don't you two join me and Margot on the barge, and Sashay, bring your sail."

Magritte climbed back into the helicopter with his precious cargo and Dizzy popped his head out of the chopper door.

"Hang on, superstar, I'm coming down to take you two back to the harbour."

A short while later, Leo and I sat huddled under blankets on a dock in the Marseille harbour, drinking *chocolat chaud* and waiting for the others to return.

"Better than Orangina?" I asked Leo.

"Mmm, *absolument*," he said and put his arm around my shivering shoulders. I suddenly forgot about being cold.

It was a strange sight, one that would have been very hard to explain if you didn't know the events that led up to the moment. DeFaux, wrapped in Sashay's paisley scarf, and secured in a red lifebuoy, was suspended in a heavy-duty fishing net from a hoist attached to the rear of the barge that Margot and Blag had commandeered. Blag was at the wheel, singing an extremely off-key duet of "Pain Hurts" with Rudee while Margot stood at the bow, proudly holding a fishing rod at her side. DeFaux looked as glum as might be expected, and I'm sure his mood wasn't improved by the tiny crabs nestled into his goatee. I guess that's what happens when you mess with Mona!

Twenty-Seven

The crowd assembled in the square in Marseille, where it was mercifully warmer than it had been at the time of the launch of the Rally de Taxi two days earlier. Was it really two days ago? It felt like a half a lifetime to me. Leo and I sat beside Margot and Blag in a row with the other Partypoppers and Marauders drivers as the grandmaster hauled himself up onto the podium. The crowd, knowing what was to come, was subdued in its reaction, unlike the one at the launch of the event.

"How do you spell bogus?" muttered Blag to no one in particular.

"Congratulations to this year's winner of the Rally de Taxi, the Champagne Supernovas. To accept the award, here is their captain, Anatole Belmondo."

Holding a bottle of bubbly in the air and waving to his group of loyal followers, Belmondo milked the moment, bowing, accepting bouquets of roses and tossing his sunglasses into the crowd like a rock star with a bad tan job.

"I'd like to put a tarantula in his pudding," said Margot.

Leo gave me an eyebrow signal and we quietly slipped away while Margot, Blag, and the other drivers expressed their discontent with the Supernovas' victory.

"So, *Maman* is very curious as to how you managed to get to Saint-Paul de Vence after being so far behind in the race on day one," said Leo with a sly smile.

"Ahh, *oui*, a good question," I replied, "but of course, you'll understand if our shortcut remains a little team secret of the Partypoppers."

"Of course, Mac."

"And the herd of sheep blocking the road," I looked questioningly at him, "merely a random event favouring the mighty Marauders, I suppose?"

"Hmmm," he hummed contemplatively, "very difficult to say. Sheep are such unpredictable creatures, you know."

"Yes, I imagine. And that freak fog that derailed the Supernovas ... who could have foreseen that?"

"Truly bizarre, I agree," he replied thoughtfully. "And what could be harder to forecast than the weather in the south of France?"

"And just for the record, how did you get underneath the tarp on DeFaux's boat?"

Leo smiled. "I wasn't going to let that cretin make off with you just after we'd met. When he saw you in the boat, he slowed ever so slightly and I grabbed a rope dangling in the water. And when you made your grab for his cane, I hauled myself out of the water and under the tarp."

"Well, I'm very glad you did." I sounded so awkward. "And thank you."

Leo pushed his curls out of his eyes and looked at me without saying anything for a long time. "When you cut that fuel line with your friend's bracelet ... you were my hero, Mac."

I looked everywhere but back at Leo. Then he took my hand and kissed it.

"You know, there's a big party tonight to celebrate catching the art attacker. And you're the guest of honour, Mac."

What would I tell Penelope?

The Bar de la Marine was the scene of the traditional party to wrap up the Rally de Taxi, and this year's event was huge, given the national focus on the art attacker. DeFaux had been dispatched to a local jail, awaiting transportation to Paris in the morning. I almost felt sorry for him, having to get by in some damp, grubby quarters in a Marseille police station without his beloved Louis the Sixteenth furniture and his fancy booze, but I soon let that thought go as the party got underway. The TV lights shone brightest on the supposed rally victor.

"Monsieur Belmondo ..." Louise was once again interested in the results of the rally, a little too interested, I thought. "Your victory was, to say the least, unconventional. How did it come about?"

Belmondo shrugged with false humility. "What can I say, Louise, sometimes destiny takes over and leads us to places we dared not imagine. Like here. Tonight. And for me, just to be speaking with you."

Louise fluttered her eyelashes but tried to maintain her professional demeanour.

"But Monsieur Belmondo, your team appeared to have been eliminated from the rally and then, *voilà*! You were the winners. Quite a turnaround, *non*?"

"I must express my utmost respect for the drivers from the Bordeaux Bombes, the Parisian Partypoppers, and the mighty Marseille Marauders, who somehow fell just shy of achieving victory. I also offer my eternal gratitude to my spiritual advisor, Dr. Etienne Brouillard, who unfortunately could not be here tonight to share this moment of glory due to a previous commitment at an all-you-can-eat *fois gras* festival in Alsace."

Louise seemed to find this fascinating as Belmondo winningly ran his hands through his hair.

"More on this incredible victory later, but back to you, Stephane."

Louise turned away from the camera and stood very close to Belmondo, who was clearly enjoying his moment of glory.

"You know, Monsieur Bel ... may I call you Anatole, I love your team uniform, and the helmet with the bubbles says so much about the man wearing it, if I may be so bold."

"Perhaps we could rendezvous a little later, Louise," Belmondo cooed. "You know, I've always enjoyed your news reports for so much more than just the news. Your smile, and perhaps especially, your hair…."

At this point Louise noticed that the camera light was still on and hastily made a the "cut" sign with her hand on her throat, too late, unfortunately. The nation had observed the previous exchange.

Margot and Blag were watching this on the TV at the bar and clinking glasses, laughing raucously. Just then there was a commotion as a pair of gendarmes escorted Magritte into the bar with much pomp, accompanied by my parents!

How much did they know? I saw my mom's beaming expression. Not much, it would seem.

Mom rushed over and embraced me, giving me little Parisian air kisses. When my mom commits to a cultural experience, she goes all the way.

"*Bonjour, ma petite*," my dad jovially called out, although it sounded more like "banjo appetite." Fortunately, I was used to auto-correcting Rudee, so this was no problem.

"We had to surprise you, Mac," said my mom, holding my shoulders in that "look how you've grown" style. Well, it had been a whole two days since I'd seem them. "When we saw the gorgeous view from the train of the south of France I was so jealous of you cruising through the countryside, letting the breeze blow through your hair, stopping for Camembert and a baguette and chatting in your perfect French with the locals."

"Well, it was kind of like that, Mom. Although I think that baguettes may be out of season. But definitely lots of breeze." I thought about my ride in the motorcycle sidecar.

"And the fog in the harbour looks so mystical, doesn't it, sweetie?" My dad gave me his best dad hug, this time with a look of sympathy. "Sorry you guys didn't win the rally. I guess the competition was pretty tough." He grinned and nodded toward Belmondo, who was taking a victory lap of the room.

The din level was building when a squawk of feedback got everyone's attention.

"*Allo*, merry crackers!" Who else? Rudee grabbed a microphone on a tiny stage with a little keyboard. "Congratulations to the bubbleheads on their victory in the taxi rally." Was this meant to be sarcastic? "But next year, watch out for the Partypoppers zooming to victory!" A roar went up from the Paris contingent and was met with an equally enthusiastic "Noooo!" from the Marauders camp, joined by their local supporters. Musical instruments appeared and The Hacks assembled on the crowded stage. In the midst of the mayhem, Magritte approached me and extended his hand.

"You have, once again, Mademoiselle Mac, my gratitude, and indeed that of the art-loving populace, who when faced with the drabness of daily existence, look to the timeless works of the creative spirit that lives within all of us, but finds its fullest flowering ..."

I hope Magritte didn't see my eyes glazing over. It was pretty dark in the Bar de la Marine.

"I'm sure you understand why, for security reasons, your most considerable contributions to the apprehension of the art attacker must remain unrecognized publicly."

"Of course, Inspector Magritte," I said. "I just did what any kid would do."

Magritte smiled and extracted a small box from his raincoat. Tipping his bowler hat to me, he silently handed me the box. I looked around, and since no one seemed to be taking note of our little exchange, I opened the box and there was the Stella mini Fossil watch that had appeared on Mona Lisa's wrist.

"It was among DeFaux's effects," said Magritte, "and it would just collect dust in a police evidence locker. That seemed like a waste of a good timepiece."

I knew where this souvenir would be going. "*Merci*, Monsieur Magritte."

A boisterous cheer went through the crowd as my dad joined The Hacks for one of their signature songs. I think it was "Onion Heart" but it just as easily might have been "Stinkbomb Serenade." Then I saw an unfortunate sight. A group of drivers from all the teams was standing in a circle clapping as my mom and Dizzy did the tree dance that I'd witnessed at Sashay and Rudee's wedding party. Why is it that every day for parents is just one more opportunity for victory in the embarrassment Olympics? I slipped out into the street, where I encountered Leo, leaning against a taxi and strumming his guitar in the cool evening air.

"I wondered where you'd gotten to," I said.

"Too much fun for me in there."

"What were you playing?"

"Nothing much. I'm always working on something new." He strummed distractedly and I wondered how he could see what he was doing with those curls falling into his eyes.

"Well, I have to go home tomorrow. It would be nice to hear one farewell song."

He hesitated and then shrugged and began to play and sing. I remember the opening line.

"There's a girl from California …"

And the rest is a bit hazy.

Twenty-Eight

"Happy birthday, Penelope. Sorry I missed the party."

"So Mona Lisa actually wore this watch?" Penelope, obviously pleased with her new acquisition, admired the Stella mini Fossil on her wrist.

"Not actually, of course, but yes, sort of."

"Well, I suppose this makes up for the destruction of a perfectly good safety pin bracelet," she smiled and added, "and besides, Gerald and I are on the outs so a bit of its lustre is gone."

"Sorry to hear," I said, a bit distractedly, playing with my nautical friendship bracelet. "I wouldn't know about that."

"I feel like there's something you're not telling me, Mac," said Penelope, her eyes narrowing suspiciously, "and I wonder what really happened on the road to Marseille."

Also by Christopher Ward

Book One in the
Adventures of
Mademoiselle Mac Series

Mac in the City of Light

Fourteen-year-old California
girl Mackenzie, known as Mac,
goes on a school trip to Paris
where she meets up with an
old musician friend of her dad's,
Rudee Daroo, who now makes a living as a cab driver.
Rudee reveals that some of the greatest monuments
in Paris are being either destroyed or stolen and that
the city is slowly becoming darker. Mac finds herself in
league with a crew of crazy cabbies and their friends as
she tries to right these wrongs. She encounters sinister,
shadowy characters who live in the Paris underground,
a philosopher gendarme, a gypsy who can dance people
into dream states, and gargoyles come to life. From
dodging her school group to a heart-stopping encounter
atop Notre Dame Cathedral, Mac needs all the resources
she can muster to help Paris remain the "City of Light."

Other Books for Young People from Dundurn

Eldritch Manor
Kim Thompson

Shortlisted for the Forest of Reading 2014 Silver Birch Award for Fiction, and for the 2014 Rocky Mountain Book Award

Twelve-year-old Willa Fuller is convinced that the old folks in the shabby boarding house down the street are prisoners of their sinister landlady, Miss Trang. Only when Willa is hired on as housekeeper does she discover the truth, which is far more fascinating. Eldritch Manor is a retirement home for some very strange beings indeed. All have stories to tell — and petty grievances with one another and the world at large. Storm clouds are on the horizon, however, and when Miss Trang departs on urgent business, Willa is left to babysit the cantankerous bunch. Can she keep the oldsters in line, stitch up unravelling time, and repel an all-out attack from the forces of darkness … all while keeping the nosy neighbours out of their business and uncovering a startling secret about her own past?

The Gargoyle in My Yard
Philippa Dowding

*Shortlisted for the 2012
Diamond Willow Award*

What do you do when a four-hundred-year-old gargoyle moves into your backyard? Especially when no one else but you know he's ALIVE? Twelve-year-old Katherine Newberry can tell you all about life with a gargoyle. He's naughty. He gets people into trouble. He howls at the moon, breaks statues, and tramples flowers to bits, all the while making it look like you did it! He likes to throw apple cores and stick his tongue out at people when they aren't looking. How do you get rid of a gargoyle? Do they help the gargoyle leave for good? If you're like Katherine and her parents, after getting to know him, you might really want him to stay.

Bone Deep
A Peggy Henderson
Adventure
Gina McMurchy-Barber

When archaeologists discover a
two-hundred-year-old shipwreck,
Peggy Henderson decides she'll
do whatever it takes to take part
in the expedition. But first she
needs to convince her mom
to let her go, and to pay for scuba-diving lessons. To
complicate matters even more, Peggy's Great Aunt
Beatrix comes to stay, and she's bent on changing Peggy
from a twelve-year-old adventure-seeking tomboy to
a proper young lady. Help comes in the most unlikely
of places when Peggy gets her hands on a copy of the
captain's log from the doomed ship, which holds the key
to navigating stormy relationships.